Praise for Warlady

Graham skillfully combines a murder mystery, political intrigue, and space combat in the intricate and thrilling second Calpurnian Wars space opera (after *Sounding Dark*). // Graham fashions an elaborate and fascinating world, complete with complex history, religion, and politics, without ever sacrificing the plot's forward momentum. This polished page-turner should hook any sci-fi fan. — *Publishers Weekly*

I love the rich, complicated world of the story, but it's the characters that really grabbed me: competent, clever, complex people, survivors who keep fighting for each other despite murder and invasion and all the rules of their culture. This one goes into the special group of books I keep to read and re-read. — Melissa Scott, legendary pioneering SFF author of more than thirty novels, winner of multiple genre awards

Thrilling battles in space, a murder mystery, a forbidden romance, and mature characters working to change their world, all set within another of Graham's fascinating cultures in her Nine Worlds, where far-future space opera meets spirituality with the flavour of classical antiquity—*Warlady* is a worthy sequel to *Sounding Dark*, and a story that leaves one feeling ultimately hopeful that maybe humans can after all find their way towards making a better future. — K.V. Johansen, author of the *Gods of the Caravan Road* epic fantasy series

Jo Graham's *Warlady* deftly moves the action in her Calpurnian Wars series to the planet of Morrigan, where politics, intrigue, the threat of war, and ancient secrets threaten not only the future of Sandrine, bodyguard to the titular Warlady, but the fate of the entire planet as well. Graham expertly weaves the personal with the political, making the fate and stakes of Sandrine's old relationship with the electromancer Jauffre as important and grounded for the reader as the fate of their entire world. — Paul Weimer, SFF book reviewer and Hugo finalist

Jo Graham combines two of my favourite things: a big galaxy and a personal story. With gently delivered backstory, deftly rising action, and a gorgeous re-romance, *Warlady* is for everyone who wants to build a better world. — E.K. Johnston, #1 New York Times Bestselling Author

PRAISE FOR SOUNDING DARK

Faith, luck, and grit propel this ambitious space opera from Graham (*Black Ships*). // Graham amps up the action, constructs a rich mythology of gods, cultures, and societies, and develops evocative characters that will make readers cheer. This pure sci-fi escape proves a fresh experience for fans who are tired of clichés. — *Publishers Weekly*

Sounding Dark is tremendously exciting space opera. // It's the sort of book you stay up far too late finishing, and then go back to re-read so that you can savor the details. The thing that's hard to express how well *Sounding Dark* blends solid technical SF // with deep myths. // Jo Graham makes both aspects utterly believable and equally crucial to the story. — Melissa Scott, legendary pioneering SFF author of more than thirty novels, winner of multiple genre awards

Also by Jo Graham (selected works):

Black Ships

Stealing Fire

The Order of the Air
(series, Melissa Scott co-author)

The Calpurnian Wars:

  Sounding Dark

  Warlady

WARLADY

Jo Graham

Candlemark & Gleam

For information, address
Athena Andreadis
Candlemark & Gleam LLC,
38 Rice Street #2, Cambridge, MA 02140
eloi@candlemarkandgleam.com

Library of Congress Cataloguing-in-Publication Data
In Progress

ISBNs: 978-1-952456-10-7 (paperback), 978-1-952456-11-4 (digital)

Cover art by Eleni Tsami

Editor: Athena Andreadis

Proofreader: Kelly Jennings

www.candlemarkandgleam.com

For Amy,

my Sandrine

CHAPTER ONE

The doors of the Antechamber to the Presence stood open, the dim lights illuminating little besides the dark red hangings. Eternal starry night-sky glittered on the ceiling, constellations mirroring those of the sky without. The man who let Sandrine into the Sanctum was a Black Guard, with a neatly trimmed mustache and dark eyes; one of the youngest members, she thought, and not one she would have picked. "My lady Somatophylax," he said, "The Chief Physician is here. And Sister Leonie."

Over his shoulder she could see the Chief Physician and his assistants in a huddle around something on the floor, the pillar of the Presence pulsing blue with striations tending toward indigo. A slight figure bent toward it, not quite touching the couch, its white leather handrests blackened. "Why wasn't I notified first?" Sandrine demanded. Her voice was harsher than she intended. "It is my place to guard the Warlady."

"Sister Leonie sent for you as soon as she arrived," he said. "I reported to the Hierarch of the Black Guard."

"And who found her?"

He swallowed. "I did."

"And you did not see fit to summon me?"

"My lady Somatophylax…."

The slight figure had unbent, and Sister Leonie hurried across the patterned marble floor, her simple gray robes contrasting with the sheen of the half-mask she wore, an open mesh of twining feathers in gold metal, a faint light chasing along them. She wore Windfollower, as she usually did these days. "Sandrine, I need to talk to you."

Sandrine allowed herself to be pulled aside, past the young Black Guard, away from the cluster of physicians. One of them looked at another, shaking her head. Their bustle was ceasing. "She is gone then," Sandrine said. It seemed impossible. "What happened?"

Leonie's dark eyes looked up at her from between the whorls of Windfollower, her voice low. "This was not natural and it was not an accident."

"What are you saying?"

"The Archegos was killed by a massive burst of electricity when she was in the interface to the Presence," Leonie said. "She died instantly. But this was not an accident. There is no way the interface could have malfunctioned this way."

"How could that happen?" Sandrine looked around her at the huddle of physicians. "I don't believe it. The interface, the most secure place in the Sema…. Why was she here? And wasn't anyone with her?"

"The Black Guard," Leonie gestured with her chin to the young man now standing alone and nervous by the door. "He was on watch outside her rooms. She asked him to escort her. And before you ask, he's a Bar-Chanot from here in Holyrood. His father was in the Guard before him, but he's only been in five months. Just enough for uneventful watch slots. She was electrocuted by the interface to the Presence itself." Her voice caught. As long as Sandrine had served the Warlady, Leonie had been with her twice as long. Leonie had been Dariah's protégé for nearly twenty years, since before Dariah had been Warlady.

"Leonie," she began.

"Don't. If you think it is your fault, how much more is it mine? I am responsible for everything in the Sema." Leonie looked away.

Her hair was escaping from its pins into its natural curls. "Someone has assassinated the Archegos under our noses and we have no idea who or why."

"This Bar-Chanot…"

"Seriously?" Leonie looked at her. "You think that boy has the subtlety to do this? No, whoever did this used the power of the interface itself. That requires a great deal of skill and knowledge. Someone had access to the interface and the ability to use it."

Sandrine took a deep breath. For some reason her voice was not clear. "Then who? Someone high in the blood hierarchy."

"I have no idea. We both know the Warlady had enemies. But one who could get into the Sema and use the Presence itself as a weapon?"

"A foreign power? The Calpurnians would do this if they could."

"And can they? We have no indication they can. Of course they have agents, but to get in here and sabotage the very Sema itself? They have no Dreamers. I don't see how they could have used the interface."

Sandrine looked away from the knot of physicians. She was not going to look at the body. Her eyes met Leonie's. "I don't know who could do that. Or rather, I don't know who could from a technical viewpoint and would have access. Have you tried to ask the Presence?"

"You think I'd go into the interface after what just happened? For that matter, this chair is completely burned out. The pads took so much current that they're inoperable." Leonie said. "And yet Windfollower senses nothing unusual. I have not tried a different interface elsewhere in the building. And no one shall do so until we find out how the Warlady was killed, if you were thinking of doing it yourself."

"I was, but I won't." Sandrine shook her head. She had to be clear-headed. She could not think of the Warlady herself, not at this time. "We need someone who can slice the interface without activating whatever the trap is." She took a deep breath. "You there! Bar-Chanot! Orders for you."

The young Black Guard almost tripped over his own feet hurrying to her. "Yes, my lady Somatophylax?"

"Send word to Sea Easting. I want Jauffre Castal-Edo brought immediately. The electromancer."

The sea beat relentlessly against the walls of the tower, the stars above penetratingly bright, a night that never ended. It was more than two thousand kilometers to the beginning of the transitional zone, far out to sea, and on this tidally-locked world Sea Easting would never see a sunrise. Jauffre rose in the darkness, as he always did. He took his tea by the window. It did not open, but it gave a generous view of the white-capped waves occasionally punctuated by the pink or red lights of the kraken hunting just beyond the rocks where the river met the sea.

His tray had a warming dish for the thick potato porridge of the daymeal, the gravy ready to pour over it, double-ended spoon beside it, one end for the porridge and the other for the tea. Jauffre poured the gravy, then opened a paper-bound book propped on a wooden stand. Electronic readers were too much of a risk with electromancers, but paper was a tried and true way to read. In any event, this was simply a romance, not something worthy of being preserved eternally, a story of space pirates and wild adventures and forbidden love achieved. Not the sort of thing that the arguably finest electromancer in the world ought to waste his time on, but at his age and rank Jauffre could waste his time as he preferred. At least if it met with the approval of the Black Guard.

Jauffre grimaced. The troubles of the day would start soon enough. And to be sure, he had arranged things much to his liking in Sea Easting, both for himself and the junior electromancers confined to the tower. None of them would go through the things he'd endured in his youth.

There was a deferential knock on the door. "Enter," Jauffre said. Perhaps the apprentice with the tray had forgotten something.

The door slid open. Two Black Guards stepped in, a woman of about thirty and a younger colleague. "Electromancer Castal-Edo?"

"I am." Jauffre got to his feet.

"Worthy, we have an urgent request for your presence in Holyrood."

Jauffre's eyebrows rose. An urgent request was a very polite way of phrasing a summons that could not be refused. "I see," he said. He could think of no recent transgression, at least not one severe enough to require a summons to Holyrood. "And to what do I owe this courteous invitation?"

Something was wrong. The young man looked at the woman, his brow furrowed. Her response was smoother. "A situation has occurred and your consultation is wanted."

"By whom?"

"The Somatophylax Dal-Vesta."

"Ah." Jauffre looked away, taking the time to carefully take a sip of his tea. If Sandrine had sent for him, it must be serious indeed. The Calpurnians testing the orbital defenses again? No, that made little sense given their current political confusion. An unpredicted political move in the College, one that made his position perilous? Or that made hers perilous? No, Sandrine was remarkably straightforward. She said she had no head for politics and she was right. He'd seen that in the last Calpurnian War eleven years ago.

"Worthy?"

"Of course I will come," Jauffre said. He gestured to his tray. "May I finish my breakfast first?" The expressions of confusion on their faces were priceless.

The flyer landed vertically in the outer courtyard of the great temple, maneuvering flawlessly between the gilded, pierced balconies alight with bright lamps. Jauffre unstrapped. It had been a quick flight despite Sea Easting being half a continent from Holyrood, though there was no time adjustment. There was no need for one. The entire inhabitable world was a single time zone since there was no diurnal cycle to confuse things. It was exactly the same time in Sea Easting as in Holyrood or for that matter nearly three thousand kilometers further west at Evening Point.

The co-pilot came around to open the door of the little flyer. Jauffre stepped down, his silver-gray leather coat sweeping on the step. He wore silver gray beneath it too: shirt and trousers, the silver sash across his chest from right shoulder to left hip the badge of his rank, tied off in a tassel of silver bullion fringe. He straightened to his full height as a junior officer in the deep indigo of the Black Guard came around to greet him. So did a Brother in the cream colored robe of the Sema. They looked at each other. "Well?" Jauffre said.

The Brother spoke first. "On behalf of the Hierophant of the Sema, be welcome to Holyrood."

The Black Guard glared at him. "You are the guest of the Lady Somatophylax, not the Hierophant. Be welcome to Holyrood, Electromancer."

Something was seriously awry. "I am delighted to be the guest of both worthies," Jauffre said. Every window was ablaze with light. It silhouetted the patrolling guards on the balconies. He felt his palms itch. One could not help but think tactically. So much energy, and so little discipline in its application. The energy flail at the belt of the Black Guard….

The Brother glared at the Black Guard. "My Lady Hierophant

has instructed that you be taken to guest quarters where you may refresh yourself."

After a flight of three hours? "I assure you, I am in no need of rest," Jauffre said courteously. "I understand the summons was urgent?"

"The Lady Somatophylax said that he was to be brought to her as soon as he landed," the Guard snapped.

"Courtesy requires…" the Brother began.

The female Guard who had accompanied him during the flight had come around the flyer. "Security requires that he be restrained before being brought into the Sanctum."

"The Somatophylax specifically said not to," the other Guard replied.

"Our security orders come from the Hierarch. They are standing orders for all electromancers."

"And our orders are direct and specific from the Somatophylax," the first Guard insisted. Jauffre stood passively while they discussed whether to bind him or not. It was very instructive. "They take precedence over standing orders."

"If he would follow me to guest quarters," the Brother began again. The Guards ignored him.

"Then it's on your head," the female Guard said. "If someone else dies, it's on you."

"I assure you, I have no plans to assassinate anyone," Jauffre said and watched them blanch. Very instructive indeed. Sandrine must be in quite a lot of trouble. "And I am prepared to report to the Somatophylax immediately if that is her wish."

"Then I remand him to you," the female Guard said. She turned back to the flyer. Jauffre nodded to the other Guard to precede him, leaving someone else to scramble after with his bag.

It had been several years since he had been in Holyrood, and forty years since he had first come here as a boy of nine, but the Sema was still as impressive. This time, however, he did not enter by

the main doors from the Pilgrim Way, but through back corridors
tiled in white and gold, mosaics reaching nearly to the ceiling,
every surface decorated with the work of hundreds of craftspeople.
And these were the non-public rooms. They lacked the grandeur
of the fire-lit First Sanctum or the eternal starry ceiling of the
Antechamber to the Presence with its shifting murals of the deeds
of the Warlord Khreesos who had built it.

"If you will come this way, Worthy," the Guard said, starting
up an ornamented staircase of green marble. Jauffre's heels were
loud on the stairs. There was a door with a Sister outside it, an
energy pike in her hands. Jauffre suppressed a sigh. What sort of
security was that if they feared electromancers? The presence of a
guard with an energy weapon was an invitation, not a deterrent.
Which meant that Sandrine did not fear electromancers, something
that was also instructive.

The door opened onto a lavishly appointed private sitting
room. There were deep couches in a plush emerald the same shade
as the walls, marble side tables on metal legs, hanging lamps with
glass mosaics of fantastic plants. A central table held a gilded tea
service. A slight woman in the simple gray of the Sisters' robes
perched on the edge of one of the couches, a bowl in her hand, the
tracery of one of the Greater Gifts a mask across her face. And yet
his eyes were only for the room's other occupant.

Somatophylax Sandrine Dal-Vesta wore the deep indigo
uniform of a senior Black Guard, a color so dark as to be almost
black, the color of Morrigan's sunless skies. Her uniform was not
plain, however—she bore the Warlady's badge of ram's horns
across her breast. Her dark hair was pinned up in a single braid,
her eyes lined with kohl, an energy flail at one hip and a blade at
the other. She had been pacing, and she looked up at his entrance,
her eyes bright with worry and unshed tears. As always, his heart
gave a little leap.

Mindful of the Sister and the guards at his back, Jauffre bowed deeply, his fist against his forehead in a sign of respect. "My Lady Somatophylax. I am at your service."

"Leave us," Sandrine said to the guards. "And put the bag down."

"My lady." They did so with sufficient speed to indicate a desire to be gone as quickly as possible.

Jauffre straightened up from his bow. Sandrine's eyes didn't leave him. "May I present the Hierophant of the Sema?"

The woman on the couch stood. She was slender with a heart-shaped face, her hair a lighter shade than her skin, a single ringlet on each side escaping from her severe hairstyle. "Please call me Sister Leonie. I have heard a great deal of you, Electromancer."

"And I of you, of course." Jauffre bowed again. "To what do I owe the honor of a meeting with the Archegos's two most trusted advisors?" They looked at each other, and Sandrine's expression gave him the final piece. "She is dead then," Jauffre said.

"Assassinated," Sandrine said.

"In the Sanctum itself. By the interface to the Presence," Sister Leonie said.

No wonder the entire place was buzzing like a kicked insect nest. Jauffre frowned. He had only spoken with the Archegos, the Warlady Dariah, a few times in public; but he had thought well of her, especially of her more controversial policies in recent years. They had made her enemies, but who could argue with her claim of divine inspiration? She spoke for the Presence. If the Presence itself required a loosening of certain oppressive laws, who might contradict it? The Warlady had proved her worthiness in the last Calpurnian War, channeling the genius of Khreesos himself. And yet another fact stood out.

"By the interface to the Presence?" Jauffre said incredulously.

"She was electrocuted," Sandrine said starkly. "When she lay in the interface."

"How? That should not be possible...."

"We don't know," Sister Leonie said briskly. "That is why we have sent for you. Someone has tampered with the essential access to the Presence. We do not know who, why. We only know how, and that seems incredible."

"But surely you have some ideas," Jauffre said.

"I have hypotheses," Sister Leonie said. "But nothing more. You are aware that she had many enemies, both at home and beyond our world?"

"I know the Calpurnians would like to add Morrigan to their empire," Jauffre said.

"You fought in that war with distinction, as I recall," Sister Leonie said.

"Such was my honor," Jauffre said with a bow so that he did not have to look at Sandrine's face. He would not cause her embarrassment for the world.

"The Calpurnians are only one enemy, though the most obvious one," Sandrine said sharply. "Leonie, you know perfectly well Castal-Edo and I fought together. Now can we return to the problem at hand?"

"Has anyone tried the interface since?" Jauffre asked.

"No," Sister Leonie said. She touched the mask she wore. "This is Windfollower, one of the Greater Gifts. It seems to be functioning normally. I have not tried to draw on the Presence, however."

"A wise choice," Jauffre said. Especially with a Gift that interfaced directly with her brain, he thought. He wouldn't try it himself. And yet that must be the reason they'd sent for him. He took a breath. "You want me to do it."

"We need an electromancer to slice the interface," Sandrine said. "And you are the best."

"In your opinion," he replied. It could not help but bring a sideways smile to his face.

"You are the one who fears nothing," she said.

"Ah. You mean you think I'm the only one who would slice into an interface that killed the last person who used it?"

"Just so." He saw the corner of her mouth twitch.

"Then I suppose I have no choice." He made a grave bow to Sister Leonie. "I will need an alternate way in. It's quite possible that the trap is localized to the interface in the Sanctum. Surely there are other interfaces. The less-used, the better. Only a fool builds a house with just one door." It was an old proverb, but nonetheless true.

"There are others," Sister Leonie said. He noted she didn't say how many. She looked at Sandrine. "The oldest one? In the Core itself?"

Sandrine nodded. "That one hasn't been used in years. There has been no need."

"The oldest would be best," Jauffre said.

"Is there anything you require?" Sister Leonie asked. "Assistance? Tools? There are Gifts…."

"I have everything I need," Jauffre assured her. He touched his temple. "It's all here."

"I told you he was arrogant," Sandrine said to Sister Leonie.

Sister Leonie laughed, then stopped short as if sorrow had suddenly caught her again like a fist to the belly. "Sandrine, would you take him down to the Core? I fear someone must speak to the nets. Rumors are spreading. There needs to be official word."

"And that had better not be me," Sandrine said. "You're far more manipulative."

"You mean diplomatic," Sister Leonie said.

"As soon as the word reaches Calpurnia, they'll try our defenses," Jauffre said.

"I know that. The Hierarch knows that," Sandrine replied. "He's in communication with the orbital stations now."

"Then lead the way."

He followed her through a series of chambers, down three flights of stairs, and into a maze of less-decorated rooms and halls until they stopped at a security door. Sandrine put her hand to the panel and it opened at her touch. The floor beyond was somewhat dusty, the room dark. Sandrine looked about for the lighting controls.

Jauffre moved his fingers and the room lit, blue worklights illuminating a tangle of cables and boxes above, an old-fashioned cradle interface in the center of the room beneath a dark pod that rose to the ceiling. The door shut behind them.

"Thank you," Sandrine said. In the ghastly light her face looked worn and tired and every bit of her forty-one years.

"How have you been, Sandrine?" he asked quietly.

"Well enough," she said.

"You don't look well enough."

"How would you look if your friend had been murdered?" Sandrine snapped. "It was my job to protect the Warlady, the Archegos. To give my life for her. And now she is dead and I do not even know how to avenge her."

"You are her military aide, not her personal bodyguard," Jauffre said. He took a step closer. "You can't be with her every hour."

"I am responsible every hour." She shook her head sharply. "Do not try to comfort me. I know my failure."

"Then I will help you find who murdered her," he said gently.

"I knew you would."

"Sandrine, you know I would do anything in the world for you."

She took a deep breath, her eyes seeking the conduits and cables above. "Jauffre, don't begin."

"Begin what?"

"You know very well." She lifted one hand, then put it back at her side.

"You have all the cards, Sandrine. You always had. Even when I was your prisoner."

She shook her head. "You were not my prisoner."

"I was. I am. You could raise your voice and have me bound, injected with inhibitors and locked away in a low-tech oubliette for the rest of my life." Jauffre glanced down at his gray leather coat and fringed sash. "I may be a gorgeously dressed prisoner, but I am an electromancer all the same, and we both know I am not free."

She turned away, pacing across the room. "Dariah meant to change that. She said this was not what was meant when the blood hierarchy was founded. It was not what the Presence wanted. It was not what the gods wanted." She shook her head. "I agree. I have always been a heretic. Dariah sought to make heresy canon. She said we had come too far from the will of the gods, and that the Presence was working through her to change that. I believed her."

"Many people have a lot to lose from change," Jauffre said. "The powerful do not like to share power."

Sandrine turned. "And many people have a lot to gain."

"That is true," he said. "I don't want to see the young ones in my charge grow up as I did. Her reforms have made it much easier. But they don't go far enough."

"They would have." Sandrine snapped. "Change is not easy. But each year she went farther. Each year she made more enemies. Things were changing."

"But not fast enough for us."

"No," she said simply, and the regret in her voice made his chest ache.

Jauffre took a deep breath. "Then I will help you however I can," he said. "At the very least, the interface to the Presence must be open."

"It must be open when the College assembles to lay her to rest," Sandrine said. "They must elect a candidate to be presented to the Presence. A new Archegos must be elected to preside over her funeral."

"To be presented," Jauffre said thoughtfully. "By going into the interface?"

"Yes, the College elects after deliberation, then the candidate goes into the interface. If the Presence accepts them, they become the new Archegos. If the Presence rejects them, the College elects another candidate until they find one who is acceptable." Her eyes met his. "What if they tampered with the selection?"

"They might," Jauffre said. "They might try to change the criteria by which the Presence selects."

"That's not possible," Sandrine said. "The Presence is a soul. A daimon. It's not a thing that can be reprogrammed."

"But the interface can be." Jauffre steepled his hands together. "The interface could reject or even kill a candidate. Don't tell me it can't. It killed the Warlady. It could selectively kill her successor as well. Unless that successor were someone who wanted to maintain the status quo."

She nodded grimly. "That is exactly what I was thinking. Which means we have a great deal more to worry about than the Calpurnians."

"Who will absolutely take advantage of the absence of a Warlord or Warlady," Jauffre finished. "But not immediately. It will take time for word to reach them and time for them to move starships. We have some time."

"Four or five days," Sandrine said. "Perhaps more, but I wouldn't count on it."

He looked at her. "If we are still in this situation then, you'll need the electromancers."

"Of course." The corner of her mouth twitched. "I know what electromancers can do in a space battle, remember?"

"I remember well, my light," Jauffre said. *Side by side and back to back, the chaos of a boarding party, the steel gleam of her blade as lightning arced from his fingers....*

"Jauffre...."

"I know." He drew himself up. "So, now I try the cradle. And see if it kills me."

"Don't take any unnecessary risks."

She was afraid for him now, imagining him burned as the Warlady had been, but waiting would make this no easier. "I know my work," he said. "The best, remember?"

"I do," she said. She went and stood behind the cradle, not quite touching it. "I'll be here."

"At least you could dust it off," he said. "I'm wearing light gray."

Sandrine looked around. "With what? You are so vain."

He'd made her smile. "Then I suppose I'll dare the dust." He sat down on the edge of the old-fashioned cushioned couch, then swung his feet up and lay back, not quite resting his fingers on the gel pads on each arm. There was no charge built that he could feel, but then nobody expected this interface to be used. Which didn't mean it wouldn't be lethal. Just that perhaps he could get free if it were. Perhaps the pathways in his brain were as fast as those in the Core. Very deliberately, Jauffre closed his eyes and slid his fingers into the gel.

Connection. Sudden, intense, a moment of disorientation, like falling.

He stood in bright sunlight, the intense brightness suddenly blinding. Beneath his feet, sand dunes rolled to the horizon like ocean waves under the red sun. He was on the Light Side. Or at least in a projection of the Light Side, its reflection in the circuits of the Core. Heat beat at him. Winds lifted fine particles of sand, slapping him with them, his gray coat flapping. A shadow crossed him. Above, enormous cumulous clouds gathered, systems fed by the evaporation of the distant sea. Jauffre straightened up against the wind. He must be in an imagining of somewhere near the western transition zone. Or perhaps this was an actual feed from some probe or weather station out in the desert. In any event, he understood the Core's logic.

"I need to go to the Core," he said aloud. There was a faint shimmer, but the scene did not change. Will was power. "I am in the Core." The hot wind pulled at him. The clouds moved overhead, towering banks of moisture that would never fall on this parched land.

"Initialize external sensors for the interface in use," Jauffre said. This should bring up a readout of the couch he was currently in, or perhaps even a camera view of the room. Nothing happened. Jauffre took a deep breath. There was no danger, nor even a mental analog of danger. He simply seemed to be standing in the view from some distant weather station, irrelevant but hardly lethal.

"Is this the only external sensor you can access?" Jauffre asked aloud. Nothing happened. Which suggested that it was. Someone had locked the access. The Core itself could not reach out. The Presence could not reach out. He'd never heard of such a thing, and yet that was the logical conclusion. Time to test the parameters.

"Give me the temperature for my current location." It was certainly extremely hot. There was no reply. "So you are not capable of data transfer?" Jauffre asked.

There was a movement on the sand ahead. A snake made its way sideways down a dune, its shifting scales glittering, poisonous and deadly. "Snakes are not death in dreams," Jauffre said. A symbol of danger, perhaps. A symbol of wisdom? He stood and let the snake approach. It raised its head, hood spreading. Warning. Danger. He could end program. "Show me," Jauffre said. Gods cannot be bound.

The snake turned, slithering away across the shifting sands. After a moment, Jauffre followed. The sun beat down, the heat incredible. He could feel his skin burning in just a few minutes, rivulets of sweat running down his face. He climbed a dune, his heeled boots sinking deep in the shifting sand.

Lightning flashed overhead. The clouds were building up a charge he felt as a prickling along his back. They flowed eastward, toward the transition zone. Lightning flashed from cloud to ground far ahead, illuminating something silhouetted against the horizon. Ruins, a temple destroyed, columns standing against the agitated sky.… There was a pillar of light, blue shifting to indigo.

"The Presence," Jauffre said. This was not a physical place, not anymore. He took a deep breath, thinking his words through. "Kalos Daimon," he said, "Beautiful Presence, I come to you with humility and sorrow to discover what caused harm to your servant, the Archegos Dariah, Warlady of Morrigan. Please help me in this task or let me pass from this place if it is not your will." He started down the hill.

The sand dragged at him. The pillar glittered, distant and impenetrable. He started up the next hill and paused at the top. It was the same hill. He started down again. Then he climbed the next one. The temple shone in the distance, unchanged.

"You are telling me that I cannot access the Core this way," Jauffre said. "No matter how I try, I cannot come nearer." The wind freshened, almost cool in its speed. The clouds were rushing eastward, caught in the jet stream, their tops flattened into anvils of moisture.

"Who has done this to you?" Jauffre asked, though he did not expect an answer. Nor did he receive one. Instead, there was the familiar prickle of a surge, the hair on his arms standing on end, current rushing through his body. Almost too much, almost too strong, a near-strike of lightning flashing down from the clouds.

Jauffre threw his hands up, palms out. "No!" Discharge. It bounced off his palms, a blinding white flash followed by indigo, the world going dark.

"Jauffre!" Sandrine's voice pulled at him over the ringing in his ears. "Jauffre, can you hear me?"

"Yes," he said. He shook his head to clear it. The smell of smoke filled his nostrils.

"Are you all right?" Her arm was under his, pulling his hand away from the gel pad, dragging him to his feet. His knees shook. He still saw spots before his eyes, but they were taking on color and shape.

"Yes," he said. "Overload. But I'm not hurt."

"I thought…."

"I'm not hurt." He closed his eyes. Yes, overload. He'd overloaded before when he was much younger. This was what it felt like. The current passed through, directed outward, doing no damage along the way. His body was meant to take it.

"You slagged the interface," Sandrine said. He could feel her arm like steel beneath his.

Jauffre opened his eyes. The cables around the cradle were smoking, the gel pads blackened and completely burned out where his hands had rested. The black shapes of his palms were burned into the leather. "That's unfortunate," Jauffre said somewhat breathlessly.

"You idiot! You could have died!" Sandrine snapped. "You would be dead like…" She stopped abruptly. He could imagine all too well the scorched body she'd seen, the body of her friend and mentor.

"I'm not dead," Jauffre said. "Electromancer, remember?" If the world was still tilting a little, there was no need to mention it. If he held onto her, it surely wasn't to hold him up. Her shoulder was very strong under his, nearly his height and more muscled. If he bent his face to rest against her hair, it was accidental, surely.

"Jauffre."

"I'm well," he said. Her hair smelled of smoke. That was familiar. "But it's worse than I thought. This wasn't a trap for the Warlady. This is a trap for the Presence itself."

Chapter Two

Sandrine helped Jauffre up the stairs, but he shook off her arm before they entered the public gallery. There were guards in front of the Archegos's private sitting room and on the landing across. She understood exactly why a show of confidence was required. People were already upset enough. Frightened people did unpredictable things.

So it was that the Somatophylax and the electromancer Jauffre Castal-Edo proceeded along the gallery side by side in perfect step, a dark gaming piece and a light on the checkered floor. The Sister at the entrance to the private sitting room let them in without comment. "Where is the Lady Hierophant?" Sandrine asked.

"She has stepped out to speak with someone," the Sister replied. "She said she would return shortly. Shall I put through messages from the Black Guard if anyone inquires?"

"Of course." Sandrine motioned for Jauffre to precede her through the door. "Will you ask someone to bring a luncheon setting for three? It is almost time for the daymeal, and it was an early morning." One could call the middle of the night an early morning.

The Sister almost smiled. "Of course, my lady Somatophylax." The door slid shut behind her silently. Jauffre sat in one of the deep chairs, his head back against the cushion, his eyes closed. He pinched the bridge of his nose with one hand. His dark hair had gone gray rather than merely streaked, his face deeply lined.

"Are you certain you are not injured?" Sandrine asked.

"Just a headache. It will pass." His voice was strong enough.

"I should not have asked you to do that."

"It needed to be done."

Sandrine poured herself a cup of cold tea from the set that still sat on the marble table and gulped it down as quickly as medicine, then poured herself another.

"How well do you know the Lady Hierophant?" Jauffre asked. He sat up and opened his eyes.

"You mean do I suspect her?" Sandrine shook her head. "I have known Leonie well for nearly ten years. She was devoted to the Warlady. I cannot imagine she would ever do anything to hurt her. And if she sought to depose her, all she would have had to do is allow one of the plots against her to succeed rather than stopping them."

"And you're sure that's not what's happened?" Jauffre asked.

"I trust Leonie," Sandrine said. "I know that people have evil they keep in their hearts, but I cannot believe that of Leonie. She would kill if she needed to, without malice or regret, but the Warlady was a mother to her. Leonie was Dariah's acolyte twenty years ago. No one, not even I, was more loyal."

For a wonder Jauffre didn't argue. He nodded thoughtfully. "Then who? That's the question. Who would attack the Presence itself? It's not just a power play. It's blasphemy. To try to chain a daimon...."

Sandrine couldn't help but smile. "And so you believe? You are not of the new thought?"

"I believe in the gods and that my abilities come from them, and that there is no taint to them." His dark eyes were frank. "There is no greater evil in us than in any other because our abilities take a different form. We simply have greater offensive capabilities."

"Of course I understand the genetics behind it, but I have felt the Presence," Sandrine said. "Knowledge and faith are both handmaidens of truth." She shook her head. "It was not always thus, that we vied with one another and locked away those we feared. Khreesos walked with a Navigator freely at his side. Is that not how he defeated the Calpurnians eight hundred years ago? Our fleet completely flanked theirs and arrived at a time and place for which there were no jump windows because his Navigator led them through the Void by paths which no calculation had fixed. And much as I despise the blood hierarchy, I know this because of it: I am of the blood of Khreesos's brother Argheeros, and this heritage is mine. I may be seventeen generations removed, but I am of the Warlord's kin and I have nothing to fear in the Presence."

"And we are bred to keep the abilities dominant," Jauffre said. There was a touch of something in his voice.

She had not asked before. "Have you?"

"I've made the donation four times in the last twenty-five years," he said. He busied his hands with the cold tea service. "I have no idea if any of them took or even who requested them. It's very clinical, you know. A simple matter of producing sperm to be packaged neatly in little vials, washed in a centrifuge to ensure adequate motility."

"And yet you look at the faces of every young electromancer and wonder," Sandrine said.

"Of course I do."

The door opened. The Sister on guard stood there. "My Lady Somatophylax, will you step into the communications room? The Hierarch is calling from Orbital Two and would speak with you immediately."

"Of course." Sandrine got to her feet. "I shall be a few minutes."

"I'll be here."

With a deep breath, Sandrine went one door down the gallery. The lights were bright, testimony to the diurnal cycle kept in Holyrood. It was midday by planetary reckoning. Naturally the Hierarch wanted an update. As the head of the Black Guards, he was technically her superior, though her appointment as Somatophylax to the Warlady had taken her out of the Black Guards' direct chain of command. The Archegos stood above the Black Guards, and so theoretically an order directly from her superseded that of the Hierarch. It was very theoretical. Some Hierarchs had dominated the Somatophylax completely. Others had not. She had been Dariah's in word and deed, something that the Hierarch Luca Weld-Savarin did not appreciate. She supposed that now she would return to his command solely, as whoever the College chose as Archegos would want to install their own Somatophylax. She was certain he would make that sting.

Sandrine squared her shoulders and stepped up to the video link. The Hierarch was a fine warrior and that was what was needed. If they faced an attack, she would not be the one to undermine his authority. Sandrine inclined her head. "My lord Hierarch."

The Hierarch was in his late fifties, with steel-colored hair he wore shoulder length, his dark uniform plain and unornamented. "Dal-Vesta," he said. "A report, if you please."

Sandrine pursed her lips. He could have waited to dispense with the title. She was still Somatophylax until a new one was appointed—and Dariah not yet laid to rest! "We are pursuing some leads, my lord. However, we are far from knowing who killed the Warlady. The investigation is in its early stages."

Was it her imagination, or did he seem more than satisfied by her answer? "What leads are you pursuing?" he asked.

"I had an electromancer slice an interface, but they were not able to reach the Core or the Presence. They withdrew when it became clear that the interface was compromised. We do not know how far this incursion extends. We do not know whether it will permit the College to present a candidate. We are endeavoring to determine this. We are also trying to discover how the interface was accessed and compromised in the first place." She thought his eyes tightened just a fraction. "I would like to stress that we are in very preliminary stages of our investigation. I regret that I am not able to give you any more definitive information at this time, my lord."

The Hierarch nodded gravely. "As regrettable as the Archegos's death is, her replacement and the investigation will ultimately be in the hands of the College. We face a more immediate threat from the Calpurnians when word of her death reaches them."

"You believe them responsible for her murder then?"

"I believe the Calpurnians are the main threat that Morrigan faces. As to murder…" The Hierarch shrugged. "We haven't established the reason for the Warlady's death."

Sandrine gritted her teeth. "What other reason might there be? She was electrocuted by the interface."

"Perhaps a malfunction." The Hierarch spread his hands. "You said your electromancer was not able to establish contact. Clearly the Core is not working properly. It is very old. It's not impossible that it malfunctioned. Machines do."

"With all due respect, the Presence is more than a machine."

"Is it?" the Hierarch asked. "It is certainly a very potent artificial intelligence which has saved our world more than once. But it is not supernatural, Dal-Vesta. The Core is a machine. It can malfunction. If it tragically did so…." He let the sentence trail off.

"I do not believe that is what happened," Sandrine snapped. "I believe it was tampered with so that it would kill the Warlady."

"You believe, Dal-Vesta," he said. "That is not proof. It seems to me that it's more likely that a very old machine malfunctioned than that some nefarious person tampered with a highly secure system to plot murder! In any event, the Black Guards' job is to protect Morrigan. This matter is the business of the College. There is no need for you to investigate further. I expect you to maintain security in the temple and await the arrival of the members of the College. Is that clear?"

"Yes, my lord," Sandrine said through clenched teeth.

Sandrine returned to the sitting room to find a dark-haired girl in the cream tunic and leggings of an acolyte of the Sema unpacking a three-tiered gilt cart while talking to Jauffre. He was sitting forward on the edge of the chair and talking animatedly as the girl poured a day-tea into the bowl between his hands. "Many thanks and gracefully done, acolyte."

"This is Elen," Sandrine said, sliding onto the sofa opposite. "I will have some too, if you please."

"She introduced herself," Jauffre said. "And provides excellent service." And that was Jauffre all over, busily charming everyone he came in contact with. Sandrine had spent months around him before she had recognized it as the defense it was; if he was well-liked, it was harder to punish him. It was only the presence of Elen that prevented her from saying, *You are as manipulative as Leonie.* Instead she said, "You and Leonie must have a charm competition."

"Speaking conjures me like a spirit," Leonie said, coming into the room and letting the door slide shut behind her.

"My Lady Hierophant," Jauffre said, starting to get to his feet, but Leonie motioned him to sit. The girl had drawn herself up beside the cart as was proper for an acolyte when the Hierophant entered, and Leonie turned to her. "Elen, I am sending Gilliane and Rafeo out of Holyrood. You are to go with them."

The acolyte's respectful demeanor vanished. "Raf is eight years old!"

"So he is, and you are but sixteen."

Elen lifted her chin. "Are you sending all the acolytes away, or just those related to you by blood?"

"I am sending the one who can be used as a hostage against me," Leonie snapped.

"I won't go and leave my friends in danger because I am your daughter and they aren't."

Leonie looked at Sandrine. "When did she become so defiant?" Sandrine shrugged.

"I have a mother who taught me about loyalty and doing what is right," Elen said. Jauffre made some noise that turned into a cough. He took a quick sip of his tea.

"Endgame," Sandrine observed.

Leonie shook her head. "Very well. You can stay for now. But if I order you to leave as the Hierophant, not as your mother, you must obey."

"I understand," Elen said.

"Then get out of here," Leonie said. "We can serve ourselves and we have much to discuss which is not for your tender ears."

"Yes, mother," Elen said with a quick smile. She bent and kissed Leonie's cheek, taller than her by ten centimeters.

"Leave the cart," Sandrine said. She busied herself with the serving pieces while the door shut behind her, putting the covered dishes of stuffed bread on the low table between the couches. She had not eaten since the previous day, and hunger came upon her suddenly. It had been that way during the war—as soon as grief and horror waned the needs of the body came flooding back.

"Your daughter is delightful," Jauffre said politely to Leonie.

"My daughter is a menace," Leonie said. "Now tell me what happened when you tried the interface."

They took turns telling her while they ate, and then Sandrine related her conversation with the Hierarch. "He told me to do nothing," Sandrine said. "To simply leave it to the College!"

"The College is not going to do anything soon," Leonie said. "It will be tomorrow before they are all here, much less go into session. There will be panic, posturing, arguments…. Whoever has done this will have ample time to cover their trail."

"And there are the Calpurnians, which will certainly cause a distraction," Jauffre said. He was putting away his third piece and the color was better in his face.

Sandrine snorted. "They cause a distraction even if they are not here and do not come."

Leonie steepled her hands. "My sources tell me that they are in considerable political disarray since the death of Altissima Gnea. It's possible they will attack, but far from certain. But you are correct: the specter of their presence is almost as effective as their presence itself."

"You're getting at something," Jauffre said.

"Just observing that a panic about the Calpurnians is the most effective way to shut down an investigation."

"And when a new Archegos is elected, if it is someone who was behind the murder, they will make certain that an investigation goes nowhere," Sandrine said. "That must be the reason for it. To replace the Warlady with someone with different views. She had made many enemies."

Jauffre shook his head. "It's more than that. It's an attack on the Presence itself."

"Presumably the Presence could tell us what happened," Sandrine said. "Isn't that obvious?"

"Then it's not just a matter of stalling an investigation until someone with different politics is elected. The Presence must never be allowed to speak again," Jauffre said.

Sandrine felt a cold chill run down her back. "To destroy the Most Holy Sema…"

"…cannot be allowed," Leonie finished. "I am the servant of the Presence."

"There are those who would say that destroying the Sema would be an act of brave rebellion," Jauffre observed. "Who believe that it is simply a very old AI that holds us all in thrall to its pronouncements."

"You do not believe that," Sandrine said.

"I don't. But there are many who do." Jauffre replied, his eyes unwavering on Leonie's. "What do you believe? You are the Hierophant and surely know better than most."

"The theological argument over whether the Presence is the soul of the Warlord Khreesos and thus a daimon, or whether it is the god who watches over the people of Morrigan is centuries old," Leonie said. She took a breath. "There is the argument that it is neither, but simply an echo, a ghost in the machine as it were, an AI which has learned to respond as if it were Khreesos and perhaps believes it is. But these are things that priests whisper about. It makes no difference to the lives of average people what the essence of the Presence is."

"It makes a difference what its pronouncements are," Sandrine said. "A great many people do not like what the blood hierarchy has become. We do not like it and we have benefitted greatly from it."

"Some of us have," Jauffre said mildly. "I wouldn't call it entirely beneficial."

"It was not always this way," Sandrine said. "It does not have to be."

"Which is how Dariah angered so many," Leonie said. "When our ancestors came to Morrigan, it was the smallest group of the human-settled worlds. If we had not carefully bred for genetic diversity, we would not have survived. Choosing one's life companion needed to have nothing to do with who contributed genetic material to one's embryos. We had already been thus for centuries when the blood hierarchy was created to preserve and optimize the greatest abilities."

"Which is why they still exist here, and we still need it," Jauffre said.

Leonie nodded. "Most of the Nine Worlds have lost those gifts entirely. There is no one who could use the interfaces of the old Navigators; or if those genetic combinations recur through chance, the person never knows that they could use them because they will never in their lives encounter an interface. We know where to look for the gifts and those with the ability have every opportunity to learn to use them. I was identified as a Dreamer when I was four years old. I have never feared the interface or been without it."

"And then there are the electromancers," Jauffre observed.

"Whose gifts are even more extreme than those of the first generations, if I read the texts correctly. It was only eight hundred years or so ago that electromancy was recognized as a separate discipline," Leonie said.

"And later still that we began to lock them up," Sandrine put in hotly. "Which is unnecessary and counterproductive."

"We are deadly," Jauffre said. "And become more so with abuse. It does not improve a dog's temper to lock it away and beat it if it howls."

"We do not lock up Dreamers," Sandrine said.

"Dreamers cannot kill you with a touch," Leonie said. "But I take your point, and you have no need to convert me, Sandrine. You know I agreed with Dariah in her efforts to ease the restrictions. You know I agreed with her efforts to broaden access to genetic material rather than limit highly desired material to those with optimal matches."

Jauffre put his head to the side. "But doesn't that risk broad inbreeding? If a thousand women request the same highly desirable genetic material, based on whatever makes it desirable, you have a thousand children with the same father and nine hundred ninety-nine men who do not pass on their genes at all."

Sandrine snorted. "As though those of us at the top of the blood hierarchy aren't inbred."

"Obviously there would have to be some limitations," Leonie said. "There can't be ten thousand children of a famous musician or military hero, even if ten thousand women would like his child. The number would still have to be controlled."

Jauffre's elegant eyebrows rose. "And what about the nine hundred ninety-nine men cut off? If you ask me, that's who would like to blow this scheme to bits. Now they have a chance of fathering a child with a woman of their own caste. If the women of their caste can aspire to the child of a famous musician or brilliant scientist, will they accept an average man's genes? The drive to pass on something of ourselves is strong. If I were an average man, I'd want to kill, well, me."

Sandrine all but burst out laughing. "You certainly are unusually modest."

"Presumably not all women would take the risk of having a child who might be an electromancer in order to optimize the chances of a greater talent," Leonie observed. "That's a cold calculation for a young woman."

"Well then," Sandrine reached for another stuffed bread. "This is academic. The question isn't who would want to kill Jauffre if everyone had genetic access. It's who killed Dariah and how we find out while we can. The Hierarch told me to stand down and stop investigating. Where do we go from here?"

Leonie took a thoughtful sip of her tea. "He can't tell me to stand down."

"You also can't command the Black Guard," Sandrine said. "You have no jurisdiction over anything except religious matters outside of the Sema."

"But I have physical control within the Sema," Leonie pointed out. "For example, I can allow anyone I wish access to any interface in the complex."

"Every interface in the Sema is probably trapped," Jauffre said. "If the one I used was inoperable, and you say it was the oldest...." He spread his hands. Sandrine thought it was his hands that showed his age, long and elegant but with too prominent veins. It wasn't fair for him to still be so beautiful to her.

"We need an interface that isn't in the Sema," Sandrine said. "There are enough of those."

"They aren't full access," Leonie said.

"It's got to be full access." Jauffre shook his head. "The Presence itself was restrained. That was what it was trying to tell me with the image of the ruined temple. The temple is itself ruined for it. It can't manifest. I need an interface that's clean. And then, yes, the Presence itself can tell me what happened. It wants to."

The door slid open and the Sister on guard duty looked in. "My apologies, Worthies. My Lady Hierophant, the Speaker of the College is calling. Would you care to come to the communications room and receive his message?"

"Of course." Leonie got to her feet. "I'll be back soon." She looked utterly composed.

Sandrine suspected that she herself didn't. The adrenaline rush of the night and morning was deserting her. "We'll continue when you return," she said.

Jauffre stood courteously as Leonie left, then sat down on the couch beside her, reaching for his tea bowl and not looking up from it. "You know it's only a matter of time before whoever set the trap comes after us."

"I know," Sandrine said.

"If the Hierarch is involved…" He let the words trail off, looking up at her from the bowl.

She swallowed. "I am demoted and you are killed. I should not have involved you in this." So close. Close enough to touch. Four years since she had seen him, and that in public gatherings.

"I know the risk," he said. "I have more to gain than you as well." He put the bowl down on the table.

"What could you possibly gain that would be worth it?" His hand was so close to hers, every beloved crease and scar.

"My freedom." He was looking at their hands too. "Is there someone in your life, Sandrine?"

"What? No. I don't have time for anything like that. I'm much too busy." Drawn together, like metal to a lodestone. Their hands touched, fingers entwined, her right and his left, skin on skin like a dance, the pressure of his fingers between hers, the caress of her thumb across his knuckles…. "And you?" Sandrine thought her voice sounded a little breathless.

"No. My social circles are somewhat limited. And I am not the kind of master who sleeps with his apprentices."

"Of course not." She lifted his hand in hers. So strange to touch him again.

Perhaps he sounded a little breathless too. "You do know that having a guard with an energy pike across the door is an invitation for an electromancer, not a deterrent."

Yes, the Sister outside who might come in at any moment, but probably wouldn't. "I don't think you're going to suddenly turn on me with a pike." She brought his hand to her lips, brushing the top of it lightly, and he turned his hand against her cheek.

"Besides," Jauffre said. "You're wearing a blade. You could best me in close quarters."

"Is that what you want? My blade at your throat?" It slipped out before she could stop it, the air between them seeming like it might ignite, his hand against her cheek. She saw the pulse jump in his throat.

"My precious lady," he said, the faintest tremor of electricity in his fingers. He drew his hand back, though his eyes did not leave hers.

"I know," Sandrine said.

"All the reasons are still the reasons."

She took a deep breath, sitting up straighter and reaching for something to move around in the table service. A spoon came to hand. It was out of place. "We have things we must do."

"Yes." His voice sounded almost normal. "How long did it take you to call for me this morning?"

Sandrine shook her head. "Not five minutes. You are the only electromancer I can trust." She had not even thought twice. Of course she needed him. And of course he came.

"And the best." There was a smile in his voice. They were back on safer ground.

"That too," she said, risking a shared glance.

"If Leonie can find an interface…" Jauffre began.

The door slid open and the Sister put her head in apologetically. "Please excuse me, my lady Somatophylax, but there are two of the Black Guard who are here to speak with you immediately."

"Admit them," Sandrine said, standing up. Thankfully they hadn't arrived a minute earlier.

One was the young man, Bar-Chanot, the other a senior watch leader. They made their bows very properly. "My lady Somatophylax," the senior said. "We are here to take the electromancer Castal-Edo to confinement."

"Who has ordered this?" Sandrine demanded. "He is under my direct supervision!"

"Our orders come from the Hierarch himself," the senior said. "His personal directive."

"I see."

Jauffre glanced at her, and she could read all in it. This was the next move in the game, to prevent him from using any other interface. For now, that would be enough. He could do no harm confined to a cell, and he could always disappear later. Jauffre bowed exceedingly correctly. "My lady Somatophylax, it has been an honor to assist you."

"Your help is appreciated," she said tersely, and watched them lead him out. Then she lifted the fragile tea bowl and threw it against the wall.

CHAPTER THREE

To Jauffre's surprise, confinement did not involve an actual cell. Perhaps the Sema didn't have one, or perhaps he was still considered a dangerous ally rather than an enemy. It was a windowless interior room, probably the lowest-ranking transient quarters, with basic plumbing behind a curtain and a foam couch that could be made into a bed. There was a plastic bottle of water and a container of nutrition bars. There were no screens. The lock was electronic rather than mechanical, a certain sign this room was never meant to hold an electromancer.

However, no doubt there were physical guards at the entrance to this bank of rooms. He could open the door easily enough, Jauffre assured himself, but to do so would be an unnecessary play this early in the game. He'd have to do real bodily harm to get through the guards. He gave himself high odds of doing so, but killing or maiming Black Guards would outlaw him. He'd be hunted without mercy. And his odds of getting out of the Sema were not nearly as good. No, it was best to wait. Sandrine was not without resources. He'd wait for her move.

Jauffre sat down on the foam couch, crossing his legs and placing his hands on his knees. There was not one single thing to read or watch, but he had no need of them. Long ago, often placed in solitary because of his intractable nature, he had learned how to make the hours pass. His master had taught him well. "Jauffre, they can always take books from you. Paper burns. Screens can be wiped. Databanks can be erased. But what is in your mind is yours for as long as you are yourself." He had tapped Jauffre's temple. "Commit what you love to memory and it cannot be confiscated."

He closed his eyes. Words came easily, filling the room with their sound, as though he spoke them for a gathered audience. "Madron Porcena of Nils/by all the gods he swore/that he should be avenged/for the proud name he bore...."

Some hours passed, plus much of the *Sacrifice of Honoria*, five ballads of the scandalous poets of two hundred years ago, and a long section of the Devotion to the Lord of the Dance (except for the bits he didn't remember). Jauffre was working his way through the soliloquies of the villainous king in one of the classic plays when the door opened. He broke off, "...was ever such a woman wooed despite her high temper and willful ways? Was ever such a woman won?"

"Who are you talking to?"

He had expected one of the guards or, if he were very fortunate, Sandrine, but not the Hierophant's acolyte daughter. "Myself," Jauffre said.

Elen's eyebrows quirked. "Why?"

"To pass the time." And it had. The light had dimmed to half. Observed night was coming. Five hours? Perhaps six?

"Are you an actor?" she asked.

"Electromancers can't be actors," Jauffre said.

"I suppose not." She sat the bag she was holding on the floor. "Neither can Dreamers."

"And you're a Dreamer?"

"Oh yes!" Elen smiled insouciantly. "But right now I'm a conspirator. My mother says she has a plan. So you're to put these clothes on and come with me."

Jauffre hesitated for a moment, but then decided that the chances of the Hierophant's daughter working for anyone else were slim. And Sandrine trusted Leonie. "Of course," he said, and stepped behind the curtain.

There was a black tunic with no markings and a long, knitted coat of marled black wool, a little too large but not bad. His gray trousers didn't look like electromancer's clothing with them. He changed quickly.

"What's happened?" he asked from behind the curtain.

"Worthies from the College are arriving all over the place," Elen said cheerfully. "It's a huge mess. Nothing is ready for them and some of them have brought a lot of staff and mother is putting the whole place into mourning and getting ready for the lying-in-state and the Hierarch is expected in fourteen hours. He's reviewing the fleet with the Nautarch, so he's out at the Belt right now. But there are Black Guards all over the place arguing with the security teams of every single worthy on the planet."

"So your mother thinks if I disappear in the confusion it will be some time before anyone realizes?" He stepped out wearing the new clothes, folding his coat and putting it in the bag. "I appreciate it, but she does know that won't solve anything except for me personally?" Being on the run was preferable to execution, all things considered. But Sandrine….

"No, there's a whole big plan. The Somatophylax will brief you when she joins you." Elen was clearly very proud of the word *brief*.

Jauffre tried not to sag with relief. "Good," he managed, stuffing his shirt in on top of his coat and sash.

"Why are you putting them in there?"

"So that when someone does realize I'm gone, they won't know I'm in different clothes," Jauffre said. He grabbed the water bottle and nutrition bars and put them in the bag as well.

"That's pretty smart," Elen said.

"Thank you." Jauffre toggled the bag shut. "I presume you have a way to get past the guards down the hall since you're pretty smart, too?"

"It's covered," Elen said, and withdrew Windfollower from her sleeve pocket. Carefully, she lifted the mask and slid it on, the sensors on the exposed ends resting just above her ears. The gold metal tracery framed her brown eyes, making her look much older. "With this it's easy to put all the cameras on loop and send a call for the guards to go to the main courtyard to assist with an incoming worthy's entourage. I can slice the Sema's systems without touching the Presence."

"See that you don't," Jauffre cautioned.

"It's how I got in here," Elen said.

"I'm surprised your mother is letting you do this," Jauffre said.

"So am I, frankly." Elen closed her eyes. "Just a minute. I need to concentrate."

"Of course." Jauffre waited, the silence seeming long around them. In reality it was a few minutes. He could see her closed eyes moving behind the mask, a reflection of what she saw through Windfollower. She would be telling the guards to report for an ordinary assignment. She would be redirecting security cameras. And then....

With a click the door unlocked, as tidily as he could have done it. "There," Elen said with satisfaction, opening her eyes.

"Well done," Jauffre said. He picked up the bag as she stowed Windfollower in her sleeve pocket again. "Lead on."

She opened the door, then glanced back at him. "You trust me to have done it right just like that?"

"I've trained many apprentices over the years," Jauffre said. "I know when to trust them."

Elen gave him a quicksilver smile. "We're going down to a delivery door near the kitchen. There's a trundle belonging to the Sema waiting. It's one of those we usually use to pick up foodstuffs in Holyrood."

"And the Somatophylax?"

"She's waiting with the trundle."

"Fair enough." Sandrine was instantly recognizable throughout the Sema. Anyone with her would be noticed, while a nondescript man with an acolyte was of little interest. It would be presumed he was part of someone's entourage.

Jauffre followed Elen through the back corridors, emerging only once into one of the main inner courtyards. Despite the lights being dimmed for planetary night, they gleamed gold behind the four ranks of gilded balconies above and reflected in the droplets of a jetting fountain at the center, its high spurts rising to the level of the first balconies and crashing back in a controlled, narrow wave. They glittered in the light of the images of the gods in each niche, the screens showing them entirely lifelike and nearly life-size, the Lady of the Void with lightning in her hands. That made him smile.

"This way," Elen said, and they went through another service door, an acolyte nodding to her as he hurried past. Despite the hour, it was as busy as he had ever seen it. "Down here." She pelted down a flight of metal stairs, plain white painted walls with green arrows down indicating this was a weather-hazard shelter. Jauffre followed more slowly, his boot heels loud on the perforated metal treads. At the bottom was another door, and Elen reached into her sleeve to pull out Windfollower.

"Allow me," Jauffre said. He passed his hand over the lock, closing one circuit, and then pulled the door open. It did no damage to the door and left no trace.

"Nice," Elen said. She hurried through.

It was a loading dock, a pair of caterpillar-treaded trundles parked beside the ramps. One had its rear cargo door open. Elen jumped down and went around it. "My lady Somatophylax? I've brought Master Castal-Edo."

Sandrine stuck her head out of the door. "Many thanks, Elen."

"Where are we going?" Jauffre asked, coming down the ramp.

Sandrine wore her usual uniform, a heavy black coat over it.

He thought that she looked relieved to see him. "I'll tell you about it as we go. Get in."

"I'll let mother know you're off," Elen said. "Good luck."

"Thank you," Jauffre said. He stooped to go through the cargo section of the trundle, slipping between the front seats and settling into the passenger seat. In a moment Sandrine took the pilot's seat, touching the control to close the cargo door. The trundle's electrical systems purred to life, the light array on the roof illuminating the loading dock brightly as the trundle pulled away from the ramp. The loading dock door opened as they approached and the trundle slowly pulled out.

It had started raining. There was a slow beat on the roof, drops running down the front window as they turned onto the road, switching back as it descended. The Sema glowed with golden light on the mountainside above, the city of Holyrood dimmed below. Jauffre took a deep breath. They were away, and with no pursuit as far as he could tell. "Where are we going?" he asked.

"There's a flyer in town. It's a commercial one, not in the name of the Sema or the Guard. It will be waiting for us." Sandrine didn't lift her eyes from the road ahead.

"Much as I'd like to think of this as romantic escapade, I presume that there is a plan?"

Sandrine gave an exasperated sigh. "You said you needed a full access interface to the Presence that wasn't tainted by whoever has set traps in the Sema. Leonie says there is one full access interface that isn't in Holyrood."

Jauffre's eyebrows rose. "I've never heard that."

"Nor have I. Apparently it's in the tomb of Khreesos."

"The tomb of Khreesos is the Sema, surely?" Jauffre said. "We speak of the Presence, we make dedications there—is that not his tomb?"

"No." Sandrine glanced at him quickly as she maneuvered the trundle slowly around a tight curve. The city lights were dimmed by the rain and by the hour. "So I thought as well. Leonie says it is his temple but not his resting place."

"I'm not following."

"When Khreesos died on his last campaign, his body was brought back to Morrigan by his closest companions," Sandrine said. "It was an enormous cortege of twenty ships, with representatives from all the worlds they'd rediscovered except Inanna, with whom he had been at war. Even the Agnen came."

"I remember that," Jauffre said. "The Empress with a necklace of gilded human skulls or something like that."

"Human fingerbones," Sandrine said. "Honestly, Jauffre! How would the woman stagger along with a dozen human skulls around her neck?"

Jauffre shrugged. "I'm not a historian. It's skulls in the play."

"The play is completely ahistorical," Sandrine said. "Not to mention absurd. Anyway, I'm talking about the real Warlord Khreesos, not the one in Abi's plays."

"Point," Jauffre conceded. "So he was brought back to Morrigan and then what?"

"His brother, Argheeros, said that he had downloaded the Warlord's consciousness while he lay near death. He was taken into the memory of his ship, *Victorious*. When *Victorious* landed in Holyrood, the Warlord's spirit was declared a daimon and transferred to the Core. Khreesos had founded the Sema during his lifetime as an administrative center and a new and permanent home for the Core. Argheeros finished it as a temple to house Khreesos's spirit, the Presence."

"But not his body."

"He feared that the body would become a point of contention among the heirs, or something like that. In any event, Leonie says that he built a tomb in a remote location that was connected by a shielded link so that the Presence could come and go as it wished to visit its body." Sandrine sounded a bit skeptical.

Jauffre put a piece into place. "Which is where the rumor came from about two hundred years later that there was a secret installation controlled by a vast conspiracy that actually ruled through the Sema by mind-controlling the Dreamers. That was discredited generations ago, or at least is assumed to be propaganda."

"There is a secret installation. However, I can't imagine how it could mind-control anyone. The Hierophant has always known about it. But the rumors of control were simply fear of the Greater Gifts. Can you imagine anything mind-controlling Leonie?"

"I certainly don't know her as well as you do, but no," Jauffre allowed. "And this tomb really does exist?"

"Leonie says it does. However, she can't give us the coordinates," Sandrine said dryly. "And you can guess why."

"Because they're in the databanks that are part of the Sema?"

Sandrine nodded. "Leonie knows that they are there, but it's much too dangerous to access them now. She remembers the general area of the installation from when she read it before but, of course, not the exact coordinates. So that's where we're going." Sandrine looked at him sideways. "Yes, it's mad."

"I didn't say that." Jauffre looked out the window at the quiet city. Only a few lights showed here and there. It was too late for any eating establishments. Or too early, if one preferred. "Call it a leap of faith."

"Faith is all I have."

"That's one thing I've always admired about you," Jauffre said quietly.

"I joined the Black Guard because I wanted to serve," Sandrine said. "I know that many young people are idealistic, but I still mean it as I did then. I took a holy oath upon the gods to serve Morrigan and its people to the best of my abilities, and I am not released. I will fulfill that oath to my dying day. It is not a matter of convenience or empty words to be outgrown."

"I know." He looked at her, her profile sharp against the rain-streaked window. "You say what you mean and mean what you say."

"Perhaps that makes me foolish as some people think. They think that I am not politically astute. But I never gave the Archegos counsel I did not believe to be true, nor failed to tell her of problems for fear of her disapproval. I gave her unvarnished truth and I have never used my position for my own aggrandizement." Sandrine's voice choked. "I think she appreciated that."

"Any ruler would," Jauffre said gently. "An incorruptible servant is a rare thing."

"I will serve her yet," Sandrine said. "I will find her murderer and bring them to justice if it kills me."

"I hope it doesn't," Jauffre said. "Not if I can prevent it."

"Well, then." Sandrine drew herself up a little. "We will follow Leonie's directions to this place, find a full access interface, reach the Presence, and free it from the bindings laid on it."

"That shouldn't be any trouble," he said, deadpan. "A day's work."

Sandrine laughed as he meant her to. "And did I mention the weather system coming in?"

"You skipped that part," Jauffre said. "More good news."

Sandrine took off into gathering rain, the flyer gaining altitude quickly despite the gusty wind. A quick glance at the weather nets showed exactly what she feared: the major system rolling eastward out of the transition zone was intensifying as Morrigan's jet stream dipped to the south. East and south at Holyrood there might be thirty-six hours of heavy rain, an inconvenience and a flood hazard in the steep mountains, but nothing unexpected. However, they were going as far west as Evening Point, and much further north. They'd be only a thousand kilometers or so from the beginning of the transition zone, in mountainous territory above the 54th parallel. She couldn't ask for a worse place to experience this weather.

Jauffre looked over at her from the second seat. "Something wrong?"

"Bad weather," Sandrine said. She wished they'd been able to take a Guard flyer. They were much heavier and better suited to strong winds than this little commercial craft. On the other hand, they were all equipped with unique transponders that would automatically log their position on Guard frequencies, rendering any attempt at secrecy pointless. With all the traffic in and out of Holyrood tonight, nobody had questioned a commercial takeoff for Evening Point with the stated goal of carrying luxury foodstuffs.

"How bad?" Jauffre asked.

"Bad enough." He was more perceptive than she would like.

"Can we go over it?"

"Normally, yes. But if we do, we'll need to log our course with the orbital stations. As long as we stay low and local, we can avoid identifying ourselves. We'll just pass from one routine transponder to another until we get close to Evening Point." Sandrine grimaced. "Which means staying in the weather."

Jauffre nodded. "And then?"

"We'll deviate from our course at the last handover. If you can shut off our transponder." She smiled at him.

"Child's play."

"That's what I thought you'd say." Sandrine reached over and squeezed his hand. It was chilly. He wasn't wearing a coat or gloves. "Oh, and there's outerwear for you in the back," she said.

"You thought of everything." He hadn't let go of her hand.

"I hope I did." Sandrine checked each of the instruments methodically. "Once we get there, it will be up to you."

"Do you have any idea what we might expect?"

"Leonie's never been there, of course. And she didn't have a diagram. There's a main entrance, which I suspect isn't well marked or people would have spotted it. So it's probably under an overhang or something. There aren't a lot of settlements that far north and close to the transitional zone."

"There are more today than eight hundred years ago," Jauffre said.

She nodded. "Our population has grown and spread. But even today, that's rough country and very lightly inhabited. There isn't a large town north of Evening Point. A few mining claims, a few homesteads of people who like living in the backcountry, and a handful of weather stations and seismic installations."

"I expect the weather keeps people away," Jauffre said. "The superheated jet stream coming off the Light Side colliding with the Dark Side's polar systems—it's terrible weather. I remember reading somewhere that Evening Point got three meters of snow in a year, and that's south of where we're going."

"It's probably sheltered deep," Sandrine said. "But with standby systems active."

He looked thoughtful. "So you need me to find it. If I can sense residual electrics in the middle of nowhere, it's probably our tomb. Or some prospector's house."

"There is that," she said.

"Or...." He frowned. "There's going to be a lot of electricity in these storms. It scrambles my sense of anything."

Sandrine felt her heart sink. "So not as easy as all that."

"I can probably do it," Jauffre said. "But it's going to take a fairly careful aerial search. I need to get close to sort out an installation from random polarizations."

"Understood. We'll just do what it takes."

They droned on into the night. Eventually she let go of his hand. Eventually he got some nutrition bars out of his bag, energy to keep them awake. Of course it was always night, but it was nearing the end of planetary night, a full circle of the clock since she'd been awakened by Leonie's call.

The fourth time she felt herself nodding off, Sandrine shook herself. "Talk to me," she said. The rain was beating against the little flyer, soothing and quiet, the instruments checking themselves constantly. "Keep me awake."

Jauffre didn't ask if they could put down or stop. "What should we talk about?" he said. "Besides sex, which I expect we'll both find frustrating in our current circumstances?"

Sandrine laughed. "Is that what's on your mind?"

"Of course not," he said. He paused, a little smile playing around his lips. "Besides, I'm strapped in."

"And that's a deterrent?"

This time he laughed. "It is to doing anything about it, my light. I think sex while actually piloting a flyer is probably unsafe."

"You are incorrigible." She checked her instruments again. Sixteen minutes to the next handoff between transponders. The rain was turning to snow, melting against the windows. "Tell me about your apprentices. Or your work."

"Ah." He stretched out his long legs. "I'm still working on shutting off missile guidance systems at a distance. We have an old guidance system we practice on from across a room."

Sandrine glanced at him. "So if someone fires a missile at us from across a room, you and your protégés can handle it."

"No one will actually give us real missiles, now will they?" Jauffre said.

"Point," Sandrine said. "And your apprentices?"

She could hear the smile in his voice. "I have five at the moment. Boral is nearly twenty. He's the oldest. Then Arlaine, Melisande, and Verla. Sai is the youngest. He's just six and a half. He's very talented, though. A sweet nature. He loves animals and moths. We've been catching moths and observing them and then letting them go. I think we're going to see if we can raise some from eggs next. You know, the big luminescent moths the size of your hand? We have them in the east."

"Yes, I know them," Sandrine said.

"And Boral and the older ones are reading all of Abi's plays."

"Of course they are." She smiled. "I hope you're teaching them some actual history too."

"In context!" Jauffre said. "You must admit Abi is the good parts version, full of battles and beheadings and spectacles and dashing heroes."

"Pirates," Sandrine said.

"Strange beasts."

"Star-crossed lovers."

"Those too." There was fondness in his voice, not regret. "And what have you been doing?"

"A great deal," Sandrine said. "You know there is far more to being Somatophylax than actually guarding the Archegos?"

"I do."

"I advise her on military matters and I act on her directives. I coordinate with the Nautarch, with the Black Guard, and with the temporary levies. I meet with the Menaechman and Freyar military representatives on her behalf and brief her on developments which require her attention."

"That's a job description," Jauffre said. "Not a story of what you've been doing."

"I have been doing a great many meetings," Sandrine said. "And synthesizing and summarizing a great many reports."

"And very little hitting things."

"Yes, I miss the fun part," Sandrine said.

He laughed. "But I expect you do it well."

"I do," Sandrine said without modesty. "It is a staff position. But that is where policy is made."

"And now it will be made by…"

"Whomever the College selects."

"And who will that be?" Jauffre asked. "Surely you have an insight."

"There are a number of strong candidates." Sandrine shook her head. "I have trouble imagining a consensus on the first ballot. It's not just a simple majority. It must be two thirds of the College."

"And with the Calpurnians looming…." Jauffre let his voice trail off. "What about the Hierarch himself?"

"He's certainly in the running," Sandrine said. "I'm sure he would like it to be him. But I don't think he would be the choice of the majority unless things changed. Remember, Dariah had made enemies, but at least half of the College still supported her. They're not going to completely turn around on her policies unless there is a compelling reason."

"Like the Presence itself repudiating them?"

Sandrine had been glancing at the instrument readings, and now she froze. "Yes, like that. If it spoke thus, or if a candidate of Dariah's preference were killed when they were presented to the interface." A horrible thought struck her. "That's the plan, isn't it?"

"It could be," he said quietly. "And who is the most likely successor Dariah would have approved of who is popular?"

"Leonie." Sandrine's voice was tight. "The Hierarch would support Leonie just to make sure she's the first to go into the interface."

"Then we must make sure it's working quickly," Jauffre said grimly.

Chapter Four

Coming up on the last transponder," Sandrine said. "The current one will hand us off to the transponder for Evening Point. We need to go dark at the exact moment that the hand-off occurs. That way the current one will assume automatically that we connected to Evening Point, and Evening Point will never have us or know they should have." She glanced over at Jauffre. "So you need to kill our repeater on my mark."

"That's easy to do," he replied. "But I won't be able to turn it back on. They're not supposed to be deactivated. I can short it out easily enough. But once it's done, it's done."

"I understand." Sandrine ran her hands over the controls. The winds were gusting high. "It might happen naturally in this weather."

"If we were stuck by lightning," Jauffre said.

"That might happen naturally, too."

"True." Jauffre didn't sound overly concerned about it. It probably wouldn't bother him at all.

"I'll turn us onto a north-northwest course toward Leonie's coordinates the moment we lose contact," Sandrine said. "And no one should be able to see us in this." She nodded at the whirling snow through the window. Visibility was practically nothing, but she was flying on instruments anyway.

"Ready on your mark."

Sandrine studied the beacon signals. "Wait for it. Coming up on handover. Four, three, two—now!"

There was a sizzle and pop behind the front panel, an indicator on her board flashing red to show that the flyer's repeater was damaged. Communications showed a scroll—*signal lost signal lost signal lost*.

"We're off their screens," Sandrine said. "Changing course now." She swung the flyer around, turning north, the rotors straining as the wind now caught them broadside. The tolerances were yellow. "Dropping down five hundred meters," Sandrine said. "If I can't get over it, maybe we can get under the steering winds." There was no mistaking the whine of the flyer's electric engines, and the flyer rocked alarmingly. Jauffre was holding onto his armrests.

The flyer tilted thirty degrees, the wind hard against the left side, rotors clawing for a grip, a stall starting, and Sandrine banked hard, trading altitude for stability. Flyers couldn't fly upside down. They were reaching the point at which she'd lose control.

Another set of lights was blinking. She fought the winds, righting the flyer in the near-whiteout, the winds howling. Two kilometers lost. Three. There had to be a calmer layer....

A mountain peak reared up in front of her suddenly out of the snow. Collision alerts sounded. Sandrine gritted her teeth as though she could pull up by will alone. There—a snag between the peaks, like a gap between teeth. There was no going over, just through. The little flyer threaded it, dark walls momentarily showing on both sides before they were past. Sandrine followed the contour down, a hundred meters over boreal forest, deep into an enclosed valley. In the valley the wind was less. The alarms stopped screaming, though the board remained lit with a dozen alerts.

"I'm going to have to set us down," Sandrine said. "I can't fly in this. The windspeeds are cyclone-level. The flyer can't take it."

"Where are we?" His voice was a bit unsteady, but she gave him credit for not shrieking.

"About one hundred and twenty kilometers north of the handoff point and three hundred or so short of our destination." Sandrine shook her head. "We're going to have to wait for the storm to pass." The valley opened out a little further down, a broad flood plain clear of trees covered in deep snow. They'd sink in that, and then ice in tight as the snow refroze. Great way to get trapped. "I'm just looking for somewhere firm to set down."

"How about there?" Jauffre pointed. Through the blowing snow the terrain follower showed a broad ledge above the treeline that was scoured almost clear of snow by the winds. The peak above sheltered it from the west.

"Looks good." Sandrine trimmed the flyer neatly, descending with a circling motion like a bird coming to rest. The moment they were in the shelter of the peak, the winds died. It was as if silence had suddenly fallen. They'd built up so gradually she hadn't been aware of their scream. She could hear the rotors again. Sandrine set the flyer down gently on the ledge and cut the engine.

For a moment they sat in silence, the snowflakes lazily hitting the windows and melting from the warmth within. Jauffre let out a long breath. "Scared you?" Sandrine said.

"My precious lady, I was petrified," Jauffre said.

"Me too." Sandrine started laughing. The release of tension was almost like intoxication. She reached over and hugged him, the straps digging into her lap and shoulder as she reached for him, just barely loose enough to put her arm around him, to feel his hair against her face.

"I'm glad you didn't tell me that," he said, his arm going half around her back.

"These belts," she said. She pulled back, catching her breath. "I know time is of the essence, but we've got to wait this out."

"Dead will do no one any good," Jauffre agreed. It was very

dark in the flyer, illuminated only by the emergency lights. Which reminded her of something.

"We're going to lose heat fast," she said. "And the battery is finite. We can run the heater, but first it will cut down our search time if we drain it too much, and second it will be a signature anyone looking for us can find."

"Is anyone looking for us?" Jauffre asked. "Wasn't that the idea of that maneuver? We have to take the risk of running the heater. As for the battery charge, I can recharge it from ambient electricity in the storm if I must. It's slow, but possible. And we need the ventilation from the heater. Otherwise we'll build up carbon dioxide in a closed cabin."

"True enough," Sandrine said. She turned the heater on, carefully checking to make certain it was drawing in outside air.

Jauffre unstrapped, climbing between the seats and into the compartment behind. He started rearranging something, possibly the overcoat she'd brought for him. It was impossible to see what with only the dim lights on the board.

"What are you doing?"

There was a smile in his voice. "Isn't this the part in the romantic novels where the protagonists huddle together for warmth?"

Sandrine burst out laughing. "You are the most impossible man in the world! What makes you think I have any idea what protagonists in romantic novels do?"

"So I'm to think you've stopped reading them?"

"I'm much too busy...."

"Yes, yes. You're much too busy for anything fun." Jauffre had arranged things to his satisfaction. She could see the pale shadow of his silver-gray boots and trousers. "I'm certain you never read adventures anymore, never go to plays, never so much as listen to a poet."

"I didn't say I never...." Sandrine began. She tilted her head back ruefully. "I live inside my head a lot these days."

"I do understand that." His voice was quiet. "You were meant for beauty and light, for the clash of steel and the urgency of blood and the passion of aftermath, not endless meetings and dishonest words."

She swallowed. "And you were never meant for a cage."

"I make the best of it. And I hate it." He shifted in the dark. "I love my apprentices, but I hate the cage."

"I know." Sandrine climbed between the seats. It was too low to stand up straight. She sat down next to him, his coat spread across the rear seat, his arm behind her. She closed her eyes and leaned back. It was so warm, so right, the wiry strength of his arm, the roughness of his chin against her cheek where his beard was growing out, her arm going around him as she rested against him, the low rumble of his voice.

Because of course he was talking. Of course he had a word for the moment. "Had we forever and a day/lady, I would not seek to sway/you from your solitary course/but time has no remorse./ Merciless, let us tear/our pleasures with rough hands/from the moments time commands."

He would have gone on another thirty-eight stanzas, Sandrine thought, had she not stopped his mouth with a kiss.

Jauffre woke in darkness, as he always did. The difference was the warmth of Sandrine beside him. She was curled against him, her back to his chest, her warm coat over them both. Clothes undone, he could feel the warmth of her stomach against his hand where it was beneath her shirt, his bare ankle hooked over hers. Jauffre bent his head against her hair. Sandrine quiet and still was a thing to be savored, these moments before everything began again.

Stolen, yes, entirely so. But as one of his mentors had said when he was not yet twenty, *if you must steal to have anything, be a thief.*

In the past electromancers had rebelled and the results had been bloody. It was easy to kill guilty and innocent alike. And who was innocent? All of society bore the guilt for their fear or their apathy. Kill everyone? There had been electromancers who thought that way. All they would have done ultimately, for all their talk of justice, would have been to establish a new blood hierarchy with themselves at the top.

Revolution is easy; reform is hard. He credited no one else for that saying. It was what he had said to the tens of electromancers he'd trained in the last twenty-five years. And were they not the core of this service now? Were not half the electromancers currently living those he knew personally and influenced? He bragged to Sandrine that he was the best, and it was probably true, but his real power lay much deeper. They trusted him. They admired him. They listened to him, argued with him, even hated him, but could not deny his importance. Frying someone with lightning was very little compared to the power to persuade them.

Sandrine shifted in her sleep, her fingers entwining with his around her waist. Natural enemies, of course. But wasn't that the stuff of epics? The ache of desire began again. There would never be enough, could never be enough, of her. And yet the winds had died down outside the flyer. They had rested. Without moving, he could see the clock on the board. They were out of time.

Sandrine moved. He felt her wake, his face against her hair. "We weren't going to do this again," she said.

"We always say that."

"And yet we do."

His fingers squeezed hers tightly. "You are the love of my life."

Her breath caught. "You say the most absurd things," she said.

He smiled. "I assure you, I'm perfectly sincere."

"I know. That's what's absurd." Her hand tightened, as though she could hold onto him forever, keep his arm around her waist through time and space. A few moments more, and then they would begin. And of course Sandrine let go, sitting up and pushing her hair back from where it had strayed from its braid. "Look at the time! And the winds have calmed. Perhaps the storm is past. We need to get moving."

"It's only been a few hours. We needed to rest," Jauffre said.

She began rearranging her clothes. "And now I will see if it is possible to take off again."

"We landed in one piece."

"That does not mean we are safe to take off," Sandrine said darkly. "And the emergency beacon is fried, so no one can find us if we cannot."

"You told me to fry it!"

"So I did. I am going out for a visual inspection." Sandrine was putting her socks and boots on. "Hopefully there is little damage. I must check all the flight surfaces." She grabbed her coat, tumbling out the hatch in a flurry of snow. Jauffre winced at the cold on too much bare skin before she slammed the hatch shut.

"I don't suppose this flyer has a way to boil water," he said. But perhaps it did. A way to make tea and to reconstitute various dehydrated food packets was reasonably standard equipment. And he certainly had electricity to spare.

There was a daymeal spread in the green salon, but no one seemed to be availing themselves of it. Either it was too early, or they had too much politicking to do, or Dariah's death had genuinely hit them hard. Leonie got a bowl of tea and went down the gallery to her office. She had barely seated herself when there was a chime at the door. "Yes?"

"May I come in?" The voice was that of Serene Tomas.

"Of course," Leonie said, and came around the desk to welcome him with the kiss of peace.

He was twenty years her senior, but lean and fit, wearing the purple surplice of the Golden Lady, and he too had a tea bowl in his hand. "How are you holding up, Leonie?" He put one hand on her shoulder.

That was a question she did not intend to answer, not from him at least. "Well enough," she said. "Considering that it was murder."

His brows rose. "You're certain of that?"

"Yes."

"But?"

How soon should she tip her hand? How much did she trust him? Not enough, Leonie thought, for all that he had always been an ally of the Archegos. "I am, but I can prove nothing," Leonie said. "I am investigating, but…" She spread her hands. "You see the chaos. I hope that I will learn something, but I cannot know that I will. So many people had so much access."

Was it her imagination or did he seem to relax a little? Perhaps it was her imagination. Perhaps she was seeing villains everywhere. Leonie resumed her seat and gestured courteously to a guest chair. "But we must carry on her work."

"Yes." He nodded solemnly. "Dariah would not want us to lose sight of her work. Loosening the restrictions of the blood hierarchy, extending residence rights to life companions of Morriganian citizens—these are things that must proceed."

"I agree." She raised one eyebrow. "Are you asking for my support?"

"I am offering mine," Serene Tomas said.

Leonie shook her head. "I can't even begin to imagine taking Dariah's place."

"Someone must," he said. "And you will continue the reforms she began. Tell me you will think on it."

"I will think on it," Leonie said. "But first we must honor Dariah."

"And find the truth about her death, if you are correct," Tomas said. "Have you had an electromancer look at the interface?"

"I have, but he could tell me nothing." She shrugged innocently. "I don't think that's a fruitful way to proceed."

"Probably not," Tomas said, and their conversation turned to other things.

Serene Tomas had just left when there was another soft knock on Leonie's door. She sighed. "Come in," she said.

It was a young Brother in an acolyte's cream tunic and leggings. "I beg your pardon most humbly, My Lady Hierophant, but there is a man here who says he has business with you and will meet with no one else."

"Indeed?" Leonie's eyebrows rose.

"He says that he has rare oils for sale." The boy looked perplexed.

"Bring him up immediately," Leonie said. It was a passphrase, of course, one used by her most unusual sources.

"As you say, My Lady Hierophant." The boy bowed his way out. Leonie paced around her desk. Tea. She would tell the boy to bring more. There was no voice-activated system in her office as a security measure. Leonie was very careful about such things, given that almost every room in the Sema was no doubt surveilled by any of ten factions. She was one faction herself, but she was the authorized one.

The door opened again, the boy courteously standing back for the visitor. "Thank you," Leonie said. "And please bring us a tea service for two. We will be negotiating for some time." The door slid closed, the boy off on his errand. Leonie smiled at her visitor, for he was indeed one of her favorites. "It's good to see you, Captain Perisad."

Perisad was trim and slight, shorter than Leonie herself, who was not tall. His weathered face broke into a smile. "And to see you, My Lady Hierophant."

"Please have a seat," Leonie said. "I presume you came in good time for a reason."

"Only to find the world in turmoil," Perisad said. "The Warlady murdered? That's the rumor anyway. News of her death traveled as fast as the first ship off Morrigan after it happened, but murder… that news had not reached me. Is it true?"

"Yes," Leonie said. "Culprit still unknown."

Perisad shook his head. "There's a bad business."

"It is indeed." She waited.

"There is a Calpurnian fleet amassing at Cassandreia." Perisad leaned forward. "I came here by the fastest route, a long jump direct from Cassandreia, thirty-two minutes in the jump so you'd know." That was indeed a long jump, and potentially harmful to both ship and crew, but it cut out the usual time wasted jumping from one intermediate point to another and waiting for jump windows in between. "You're not surprised."

"I'm not surprised the Calpurnians will try us, with the Archegos dead. I'm surprised they're underway this soon," Leonie replied. "Who is in command?"

"The word is that Altissimus Iulus is taking personal charge," Perisad said. "He's all but sewn up a ruling coalition since Altissima Gnea was killed. Now he needs a victory to seal it. Taking Morrigan would be that victory. Gnea and Cordelius tried it eleven years ago and were repulsed. Doing what Altissima Gnea couldn't will essentially mean Iulus rules alone."

Leonie nodded slowly. "How long do we have?"

"They're waiting for ships to assemble." A quick smile crossed his face. "They lost so many at Eresh they've got to pull them from all over. A couple of days? Maybe three or four depending on what stations they're getting them from and what the jump windows look like from each point."

"And then how long till they're here?"

"My Lady Hierophant, I couldn't begin to guess. I haven't run the numbers on jump windows from Cassandreia for a few days from now. But I do know this: Altissimus Iulus has the reputation for being an aggressive commander. He'll use the long jumps to avoid the fleet having to coordinate coming in and out of jump two or three times. Even if that means a forty-minute jump direct from Cassandreia."

"A forty-minute jump will leave half his crew blathering," Leonie said.

"Not if they jump sedated."

Leonie steepled her fingers. "And go into battle sedated when they arrive?"

"I don't think he's expecting much of a fight, with the Warlady dead and all."

The door opened, the boy returning. He carefully placed the tea service on Leonie's desk, bowls and warming tray and pot, pierced porcelain spoon and ramekin of dried leaves and flowers tied with their own dried stem.

"Very nice," Leonie said. "We will serve ourselves." It was a dismissal, and the boy bowed himself out again. She busied her hands with the service, its ritual giving her time to think.

Perisad looked at her keenly. "Will he get one?"

"For whom are you asking?" she asked.

"Just a general interest as a free trader," Perisad said.

"Not, for example, for the Council on Eresh?" Leonie asked, pouring the water gracefully.

"I provide information to a number of interested parties," Perisad said. "But none in conflict with one another." He pressed his hand to his breast. "I do have standards."

"Then you may tell the Council that we will hand Altissimus Iulus his fleet in tiny pieces if it sticks its nose in our system," Leonie said.

"But without the Warlady...."

"There will be a new Archegos on the throne of Khreesos." Leonie handed him one of the tea bowls with a polite flourish. "Last time they tried our defenses on and off for nearly two years. They lost fifteen ships and who knows how many crew trying to get through, and never so much as managed to hit Morrigan with a single missile. We will do the same thing again if pushed to it. It would be wiser not to push."

Perisad nodded solemnly. "You'll use the electromancers."

"We will indeed."

"And will you be the chosen one?" he asked.

"That is yet to be determined. I will surely be a candidate." Leonie steepled her hands around her bowl.

"Then I wish you the best of luck, My Lady Hierophant."

"Thank you," Leonie said. "Now, how much do you want for your oils? Since you have brought them here in such haste from Cassandreia?"

Chapter Five

Sandrine stepped out of the shelter of the flyer's wing, the cold hitting her with a shock like a slap with a wet towel. The storm had blown itself out, the stars scoured clear and bright. Their faint light reflected from the snowpack, making it bright enough to see without a handlight. The ledge itself was only lightly dusted with snow despite the ravines around it where the snow lay neck-deep. The wind had prevented the flyer from being buried.

She walked around it carefully. The edges of the rotors had iced, melted snow refreezing, but they would warm quickly enough when she turned the systems back on. The embedded heaters would do their work swiftly. If there was enough power. Sandrine shook her head ruefully. Normally, that might be a problem, but not today. Carefully, she checked all of the flight surfaces. There seemed to be no damage despite the rough landing. If they weren't on a fool's errand, they'd be fine.

Chafing her hands together in their gloves, Sandrine reopened the cabin door and ducked inside. A welcome scent greeted her. "You made tea?"

"I imagine we have a busy day ahead of us." Jauffre looked smug. "Only one flask, though." He held up a self-heating electric flask.

"We'll share." She sat beside him, taking her gloves off and sipping from the flask he held.

"How does the flyer look?"

"I don't think there's damage," Sandrine said. "I'll need extra power to warm the rotors pre-flight, but you said you could juice the battery if it needed it."

"I can, but I think the charge is probably sufficient. Especially if we don't have a long flight ahead of us."

"Not more than an hour," she said. "If Leonie's coordinates are correct."

"And if they aren't?" Jauffre asked.

"Then we look." That Leonie could be wrong about the entire thing didn't bear thinking.

"Fair enough."

They took off under a cloudless sky, staying low to avoid catching the attention of the orbital nets, on a course nearly due west. The little flyer handled well, Sandrine thought. It had come to no harm. Below, the boreal forest was giving way to barren peaks and landscape entirely shrouded in snow from the storm. Either the snow was extremely deep or there was no vegetation here at all.

Twenty minutes later the snow seemed less. Deep gullies scoured the land, white waterfalls leaping cold under the stars. "You'd think they'd be frozen," Jauffre mused from the second seat. He'd bothered to put his heavy coat on.

"There's a very good reason they're not. Look!" Sandrine pointed ahead. On the horizon there was a bright streak, a glowing band behind the sharp peaks. "We're getting close to the transition zone." Jauffre grinned. It was indeed incredibly beautiful. "I grew up in the zone," Sandrine said. "I learned to fly a little hopper like this in the worst turbulence. My father had a research outpost on the edge of the desert, just outside twilight."

"You never talk about him much," Jauffre said. "I assumed there was bad blood between you."

"No, not really." Sandrine glanced over her instruments automatically. "We have nothing in common, but besides that….

I suppose he did the best for me he could. He is a very solitary man. I can't imagine why he decided he wanted a child. To pass on the line, I suppose. Both of my progenitors were kin. Or perhaps he wanted an apprentice to continue his work. I don't know. But for much of my childhood we lived alone at a research station. I took my lessons on the net twice a week. He was a scholar and a Dreamer. He was very disappointed in me when I showed no talent in either direction."

"And now you're Somatophylax."

"Yes, he allows I've managed adequately despite my shortcomings." Sandrine's voice sounded sharper to herself than she'd intended. "He's retired now. We see each other occasionally. When my work does not interfere."

"Ah," Jauffre said.

She glanced at him sideways. "What is that knowing 'ah' about?"

"Not a thing, my night."

The board chimed. Sandrine ran a query, then slowly banked the flyer to the south, mindful of the possibility of cross-currents so close to the transition. They were in the edge of the zone already. "I've got a weak power signal. Probably underground."

"That sounds more likely to be our tomb than a prospector's home."

"It's in off-limits airspace," Sandrine said. "There's a red code on it for transition turbulence. No unauthorized flights." She shrugged. "I don't actually see turbulence at the moment, though I'd guess a few hours ago it was pretty hairy."

"You're the best judge of that," Jauffre said. "We're not close enough for me to pick up a power signature from the general background noise. This close to the zone there's too much ambient electricity in the air."

"Limitations of an electromancer," Sandrine said.

"I never said I had no limitations."

"Prickle, prickle, prickle," she said, dropping lower. The flyer skimmed over the badlands. "Did you get up on the wrong side of the bed this morning?"

"Hardly," Jauffre said. "But I could have stayed in it longer."

"This is actually not a romantic escapade." The power signal was stronger now. Ahead, the sun rose over the edge of the world, dazzling in its sudden brilliance as it glared off the fresh snowfall. Sandrine raised her arm to shade her eyes.

"There!" Jauffre said. He pointed out his window and down. "That doesn't look natural."

Sandrine banked again, dropping low over the area he pointed to. It was a mountain crest, but curiously symmetrical, as though it had been carved to have six equal faces. A ledge wide enough for a light cruiser stood before it like a landing terrace. And yet this close to the transition zone, you'd have to be practically on top of it at low altitude to notice. Sandrine swallowed. "That could be it."

"What else would it be?" Jauffre said. He believed in every wild adventure, and no doubt they seemed plausible from the cloister of a tower. It never occurred to him this might be completely futile.

"Let's take a look," Sandrine said. She started the landing procedures. The little flyer settled nicely onto the terrace, its rotors kicking up a dusting of snow which pattered across the window. No, snow and sand. Some of it wasn't melting, particles carried by the storm from the not so distant western desert. It was so hot there that liquid water would evaporate in a matter of minutes.

She remembered doing the experiment as a child, she and her father emerging from the underground entrance to the research station into heat and dazzling brightness. She had poured her carefully measured beaker of water onto a plate and timed how long it took for the plate to be completely dry. By the time it was she and her father were both drenched in sweat, the glare half-blinding even through the heavy protective glasses she wore. An entire ocean had evaporated before it reached this point, rising to fall again as storms carried by the jet stream into the Dark Side, flowing through the land, rivers like arteries, until it reached the Eastern Sea. It sculpted Morrigan into something harsh and beautiful. And yet life flourished here. "Every creature seeks its niche," her father had said. "Each is perfect in its appointed place. We study their perfection to better understand our own."

"But we are not native to Morrigan," Sandrine had said. "Our ancestors left their appointed place to come here, or we would not be here at all."

"Our ancestors were led here by the Lady of the Void," her father had said. "This world was given to the smallest of the great ships. When *Starwolf* made planetfall here, our ancestors were wise. They planned the first settlements carefully. And then they disassembled *Starwolf* in orbit, bringing each critical section to rest. They brought the Core itself to Holyrood to be the heart of our systems, and that is why despite losing contact with others of the Nine Worlds for generations, we never forgot them. We knew our siblings' names and where they dwelled, and when we were strong we set forth again. We invented the jump system. Never forget that, Sandrine. While Inanna and Calpurnia forgot, we invented and innovated and created a means of navigation that our ancestors did not have. We did not just yearn for the technology of the past. We created our own."

"The Calpurnians say they created it," Sandrine had said.

"And so would the Inanni, if there were any left to say it," her father had said. "But we know it was us. The Core's memories are unbroken. We know what we did and in what year, back two thousand one hundred forty-three years to the first landing. We do not forget."

Sandrine shook her head fondly. Her father was hidebound in the worst way, and they quarreled over anything that smacked of reform or change, but he had given her the best he had, and his prejudices were those of his generation. She should visit the old man when she had the chance. He would not approve of half of what she did, but her visits gave him pleasure.

Jauffre nearly fell on his nose getting out of the flyer. The snow beneath the flyer had melted from its heat into a thin, icy slush. She caught his arm before he fell flat, looking incredulously at his silver-gray leather boots with heels narrower than the sole of the boot, curved and elegant. "What in the world are you wearing?"

"Court boots," Jauffre said, straightening up with one hand on the side of the flyer and the other one holding on to her arm. "Which are for court. Which is what you summoned me to. If I had known we were going hiking in icy mountains, I would have brought other boots. But you said the Sema, and so I dressed appropriately."

Sandrine suppressed a smile. "So you did," she said.

"I'd also like to point out that when you engineered my prison break, you sent a tunic and coat, but not a change of boots. So I am wearing the ones I brought."

"That is true," Sandrine said. "But I had very limited time, and I don't just happen to have a pair of hiking boots in your size lying around. If you'd like to fault my prison break…."

"Never, my love." His eyes were dancing. "A good prison break is always appreciated."

And there was that expression again. Surely it wasn't natural to want to kiss him standing in the slush beside the flyer. "We have a lot to do," Sandrine said.

"How long does a kiss take?" Jauffre asked. His hand still rested on her arm.

"With you, all day." Sandrine leaned in and kissed him, once, lingeringly, before she pulled back. "But we don't have all day."

"We don't," he said. He stepped back, placing his feet very carefully. "So, regretfully…"

"…forward," Sandrine finished. "Toward the overhang, I think? If there were a door from the landing area, that's the logical place."

"It would have to be a large door to fit the funeral cortège," Jauffre said. "Twenty ships, remember? And all the dignitaries and so on."

"Presumably they didn't come here," Sandrine said. "If Argheeros wanted to keep this tomb secret."

"But the sarcophagus still had to fit in," Jauffre replied. He was stepping very carefully as they crossed the landing terrace, though ankle-deep snow was less treacherous than partly melted snow. "Presuming they didn't just pull old Khreesos out and sling him over their shoulders."

"That is utterly blasphemous," Sandrine said.

"And unlikely," he said, "Which is why I point out that they had to get the sarcophagus in. So they needed large doors."

"Like those?" She pointed up at the wall beneath the overhang, enormous metal panels three times their height covered in elaborate castings.

"Ah, lovely," Jauffre said, pausing and looking up. "Utterly exquisite work!"

"Can you get them open?" Sandrine said. "Art appreciation can wait."

"Aren't you in a mood?" he said. "Snap, snap, snap."

"You're so distractible. You aren't worried, are you?"

Jauffre looked at her sharply. "Of course I'm worried. I've been worried since this started."

"If you're afraid, you needn't have come," Sandrine snapped.

"Dearest lady, when have I ever let terror prevent me from doing something I want to do?" He shook his head. "Not everyone is as utterly fearless as you. Give the rest of us mortals your indulgence."

Sandrine sighed, then took a step toward him, inclining her head to his shoulder. "I'm sorry. I'm driving you, aren't I?"

"Like the proverbial rat in a maze." He put his arms around her. "Sandrine, I know losing Dariah…"

"I can't talk about that," she said. The cloth of his heavy coat was scratchy against her closed eyelids. She was absolutely not going to cry about Dariah. Not for weeks, maybe not ever. She was not going to imagine her as she'd seen her last.

"All right." His arms were warm and solid. "We're going to do this. We've found the tomb. Now we're going to find the interface, and I'm going to slice it and we'll set things right. But this needs to be cautiously done. I need to take time to look at things and read the clues. We can't just go sailing in and grab things. So please—calmly, love."

Sandrine nodded. "Yes. Of course."

"I'm going to look at the doors and see how they open and if there is security on them before I start trying to push them," Jauffre said. "Of course they don't just open. Of course there are some measures to keep people out. Patiently. Remember, this isn't like *Golden Promise*. I've never seen these systems before."

"I know," she said. "I promise I'll be patient." She paused. "For me."

"Patient for you will be more than enough." He dropped his head against her hair for a moment. "So let's have a look at the doors."

Leonie looked around the First Antechamber of the Presence. Normally open to the public, today it was reserved for voting members of the College and their staff. The wide troughs of leaping flame framed four sections of ten seats each, magisterial chairs arranged so that they formed a semi-circle facing the doors to the Inner Chamber. Outside, beyond the flames, half a hundred staff consulted, politicked, and arranged, their colors showing their allegiances. Leonie herself wore gray as always, but the stola that hung nearly to her knees was elaborately embroidered with roses and lotuses, as was the cap that covered her hair. Windfollower rested on her brow, a symbol of her authority but also a necessary means of communicating with the systems of the Sema. Certainly today everybody needed her to do something.

She took a deep breath, smiling at the First of the Academy of Trauma Physicians who waved from across the room. All of the members of the College were here, forty leaders of professions and guilds and holy orders, with the addition of the Hierarch who commanded the Black Guard and the Nautarch who commanded the Fleet. And Sandrine, of course. The Somatophylax wasn't a member of the College, serving instead at the pleasure of the Warlord or Warlady, but was granted a courtesy seat. Her absence would be remarked on but could be explained away by the news of the Calpurnian advance. She had warned the Nautarch an hour ago. He had been on a dedicated line out since.

And now it was time. A brother sounded the massive gong three times. The College found their chairs, the muttering staff members politely quarreling over the best seats around the perimeter.

Leonie smoothed her stola. She stepped up to the rostrum at the base of the great brazier and bowed her head. "Kalos Daimon, Blessed Khreesos: we, the Children of Morrigan, are gathered together in Your name in this holy place, Your Sleeping Chamber, to elect Your heir." She did not look up through her eyelashes, and she needed no prompting text. "The Archegos Dariah, who served You faithfully, is dead. Soon she will join her predecessors in the tomb. Now, as in Your lifetime, we are ringed about with enemies. We ask for Your guidance as we choose the one who will lead us in our time of trouble. Agathos Daimon, guardian of our world, help us to choose wisely."

The murmur of assent swept through the College. Leonie opened her eyes. "I call now upon the Speaker of the College, who will lead us through our deliberations." She stepped aside, then down from the rostrum to her chair in the first row as the Speaker mounted the rostrum.

"And may our deliberations be brief," the Nautarch said. He had finally taken his seat, an aide hovering nearby, clearly annoyed that he had to remove headset and screen while on the floor. He doubtless had much to do. "The Calpurnians amass at Cassandreia. We don't have a week to chat."

And that of course set off a general babble and panic. Leonie kept a fixed smile on her face. The Hierarch stood and asked to be recognized. At a nod from the Speaker, he began. "Speaker, in light of my colleague's words, I move that we waive the opening benediction, the welcome from the Mayor of Holyrood, the Song of Dedication from the Sema Choir, and the Lustration of the Dignitaries. I move we go straight to the nomination."

Needless to say, the Hierarch's proposal was quickly approved. That created a problem of its own. If it was true that the interface was trapped, the candidate who was agreed upon and presented to the Presence would surely be killed. And yet Leonie had no proof of that, nothing beyond suspicion. Sandrine would sort it out, Sandrine and Castal-Edo, but so far Windfollower had given her no sign that they had even reached an interface, much less defused the trap. She dared not try to reach the Presence directly with Windfollower until that was so, and beyond the bounds of the Sema she had no way to contact them except with a conventional communications burst to the flyer Sandrine had taken. Of course if they were in the tomb looking for an interface, a comm burst to the flyer would be pointless anyway.

No, the only hope was to stall until Sandrine or Jauffre reached her through Windfollower to let her know it was done. But objecting to skipping the pleasantries was clearly not going to happen—nobody except the mayor was disappointed. It was two hours until lunch. A recess was out of the question this early. She had thought they would not finish the Lustration until lunch, and then the lunch recess could be dragged out two hours. That would have given Sandrine four more hours.

Leonie stood. "Recognizing the importance of what we do, I respectfully suggest we not dispense with the Lustration of the Dignitaries. Surely we all need the touch of grace so that our work may be done in a spirit of peace and cooperation?" She motioned to one of the priests of the Sema who stepped forward with a basin and an aspergillum. "Rest assured, Worthies, that we enter into this convocation with due reverence." There was no possible demurral. Leonie smiled.

Their steps echoed, the darkness barely penetrated by the light of Sandrine's handlamp. Above, there was the movement of air as though they stood in a tall space. Jauffre looked up. The ceiling was higher than Sandrine's light reached.

"Is the mountain itself hollow?" she wondered aloud.

"It seems a tremendous amount of work," Jauffre said, looking around at the carvings on the walls to either side. "For a place that would never be seen."

"The point was to honor Khreesos," Sandrine said. "And to give his wandering soul a home to return to. Khreesos would see it." Her voice was filled with awe.

He glanced at her sideways. "You believe that the literal soul of Khreesos is housed in the Core."

"I do." Sandrine raised her chin. "I have been in the Presence. I have seen the Warlady receive his counsel. Khreesos's body is dead these eight hundred years, but his spirit endures to watch over his people, and for that we revere him."

"You don't think it's possible that…" Jauffre spread his hands.

"That some other spirit or god has taken his place? I suppose it is possible. But it seems to me that explaining what we have experienced as the work of some other daimon rather than the one we set into the Core is needlessly complicating things."

"Point," Jauffre said. "But an AI that thought itself to be Khreesos...."

"I have been in the Presence," Sandrine said simply. "And I believe."

"Well, then it is a matter of faith." Truthfully, he found her certainty comforting. He had never been directly in the Presence, unless he counted the moments with the snake in the interface in the Sema, though that was no doubt the merest tendril of it, the smallest manifestation in the imaginary. He could draw no conclusions from such a brief contact.

"There are those who think the Presence is the source of all their troubles," Sandrine said. She shone the lamp ahead. "That Khreesos or reverence for the Core is simply a way to keep people trapped in their status. They do not know history." She looked around at him. "The injustices they rail against are not the way they were done in his era, nor the way that he personally did things. In that time we sent fleets out to conquer other worlds and we walked in the light of many suns, rather than keeping to our own as most of us do now."

Jauffre shook his head ruefully. "You know I've never stood in the sun, Sandrine. You've been off-world in the last ten years, and you grew up in the transitional zone. But I've never felt the sun on my face, not once."

She turned, laying her free hand against his cheek. "I know, my dear."

He smiled at the warmth in her eyes. In their shared fantasies they'd lain in warm sunlight together, windowpanes leaving dappled patterns across their skin, bright blue skies and tropical seas promising boundless freedom and leisure. Small windowless rooms had become far horizons. "Do you fancy yourself a conqueror of Khreesos's day?" he asked.

"Perhaps." Sandrine's mouth quirked. "Though I am not sure I could get used to wearing those skimpy kilts everyone wore. They seem very impractical."

"Not to mention drafty," Jauffre said.

Sandrine shrugged, taking her hand away and shining the light ahead. "We are a world with a strong privacy taboo. You should have seen me on Menaechmi two years ago. Everyone around me had just their genitals covered in silks and sequins, and I was in my blacks from head to toe. I had enormous wrap-around sunshades because my eyes are not accustomed to the light level and if I did not wear them, I would be weeping from the glare. I am sure I looked extremely stern and imposing!" She sounded amused. "I am certain they think Morriganians are odd creatures indeed."

"Well, they practice free breeding," Jauffre said. The enormous hall ended in another set of doors, these smaller but still very wide, set with mosaics of blue and black stone that glittered faintly in the handlight. "I know it's popular, but I've never found accidental impregnation that stimulating a trope."

"Why are we talking about sex again?" Sandrine said.

"Maybe because we're not getting nearly enough?"

She sounded like she was trying not to laugh. "That is certainly true! But can we focus on our actual goal at the moment?"

"I know that I find…."

"Jauffre."

"What?"

"Now you are doing it on purpose," Sandrine said.

"And you aren't? Flirting and then scolding me for flirting? You're the one who brought up walking around with bare legs."

"I was talking about historical costume." Sandrine's mouth was pursed as though she were trying not to look too amused.

"Maybe if we just spent a week in bed we'd get it out of our systems."

"You know that is impossible." Her voice was fond, not regretful.

"I know, my love." He looked up at the sealed doors ahead.

Sandrine shook her head. "And now you are calling me 'my love'!"

"Would you prefer me to stick with 'My Lady Somatophylax'?" Jauffre quirked an eyebrow.

"You manage to make that sound dirty! As though you expected to say it from kneeling between my legs!"

"Now who's talking about sex?"

"Aaargh!" Sandrine paced away, the light from her lamp flashing across the sheen of the mosaics. "Can you just get the blessed doors open without any more innuendo?"

"If you'll stop providing me with more delightful images," Jauffre said. He took a deep breath. *Focus. Focus.* He had to clear his mind. Not empty, but transparent, like water in a crystal flask. Mutable. He put his hand on the door, his eyes closing. *I am here,* he said with his fingertips. *What do you need?*

Faint currents ran through the panels, embedded fiber optic cables deep within the material. They waited for this. They waited for an electromancer. For him it was as simple as turning a key. *I am what you have been waiting for.*

The doors slid open.

Jauffre opened his eyes, putting up a hand to stop Sandrine from charging straight in. "These doors were set to open for an electromancer. Think about what that means."

Sandrine looked thoughtful. "So this room behind us was the last room that any visitors might expect to see. That means we are entering the tomb proper."

"I would think so. And there are systems active. There is a good chance the interface to the Sema is still working." He looked across the expanse of floor ahead, a corridor that turned sharply to the left. A faint blue light came from around the corner. "Let me go first. It's keyed to an electromancer. If there are traps, I can feel them and turn them off."

For a wonder, Sandrine didn't argue. There was one at the first turn: a net of detectors across the corridor, and the emitters that would run current between them like a high-voltage web. And there, on the wall, was an obvious place to put a hand, a moth sketched on the indigo walls in gold. He laid his palm against it, feeling the current moving like a pulse beneath his fingers, like his hand on Sandrine's arm. *I am here for the good of Morrigan and Khreesos*, Jauffre thought. *Let us pass.*

The system deactivated. It seemed to him that it was almost relieved. Emotion—that meant it was connected to the Presence. "It's safe now," he said to Sandrine, leading her past where the net would have spread.

"An electrical trap?"

Jauffre nodded. "Directly part of the Presence, I think. There was almost personality behind it." There was another net further on, already deactivated. "It's letting us through," Jauffre said.

"That's a good sign? I think?" Sandrine sounded less confident than she had before. Well, this wasn't her forte, not like the flyer.

"It's definitely a good sign," Jauffre said.

Ahead was another set of doors, these heavy black metal with elaborate castings. The entire door would conduct. Forcing electrified doors would be a deadly trap. Jauffre approached them quietly, then laid his hand on a moth in one of the elaborate designs that framed the central image. It knew him. The doors slid open silently.

Lights came on in the room beyond, pale gold and flickering, lamps suspended from the ceiling that held immortal fire. The room was round, rising to a dark circle at the apex, every surface covered in images. Directly beneath the center was a column of black glass resting on a black metal base inscribed with elaborate tracery that might hide controls among the decoration. Presumably inside its dark shell the preserved body of Khreesos waited. Three black couches lay before it, interface pads in each arm.

"Look," Sandrine said, her voice full of wonder. As she walked into the room ahead of him, the entire far wall lit with a glittering painting twice life-size. The Warlord Khreesos stood in the center, his Lovers flanking him. To his left stood the Navigator, his red and orange robes fringed in gold, an embroidered veil over his hair. To his right the first Somatophylax lifted his chin, blade in hand. The image of Khreesos took a step forward, lightning cupped in his hands.

Jauffre let out a long breath. "Khreesos was an electromancer."

"The things history does not tell us," Sandrine said. Her voice crackled with anger. "I have read everything. I have read all the sources, all the original ones. It is my job to study the profession of arms. And nothing, nothing anywhere, even hints at it."

"How could they?" Jauffre asked bitterly. "How could they, and lock us up? The expediencies of the day always rewrite history." The next answer was obvious. "The tomb is keyed to an electromancer because it was made for Khreesos."

"So that his wandering soul might come to rest here if it chose." Sandrine looked at the three chairs. "And so that the worthy might seek his counsel here. Do they work?"

"I expect so," Jauffre said. "Everything else does." He eyed the chairs.

She took a step closer to his side. "Which chair, do you think?"

"The center one." Jauffre stood behind it. It directly faced the dark column and Khreesos in the pixel painting behind it, still stepping forward on an endless loop, handsome and puissant, his palms crackling with power. He flexed his fingers. "This is what I came here to do."

"If this interface is trapped, too…."

"I don't see how it could be," Jauffre said. Or at least probably not, but he didn't say that part aloud. After driving him all the way here, now Sandrine seemed curiously reluctant. She was afraid for him. Jauffre took a step toward her, lifting his hands to her arms. "It will be well, my love."

"I'm sorry I told you to stop calling me that."

He smiled. "My Lady Somatophylax."

"I'll guard your sleep."

"Of course." Jauffre let go. Soonest begun, soonest over. He sat down on the side of the center couch and swung his legs up, lying back to rest against the soft padding. Then he slid his fingers into the interface.

Chapter Six

Jauffre swayed, opening his eyes and catching himself against the wall. Claxons blared, the emergency lighting blinking blue. It lit the corridor of the *Golden Promise* fitfully. Jauffre shook his head, momentarily disoriented. The *Golden Promise*, the boarding…this was eleven years ago. It had already happened. And yet the adrenaline surged in his veins, the tone of the claxon rising. Calpurnians were onboard.

Sandrine came tearing around the corner. "There you are!" she said urgently, thrusting a brown bundle at him. "The boarding party's taken the command center. Put this on."

"Sandrine…" Eleven years younger, her hair tightly braided, her dark uniform bearing the seven-pointed star of an over-lieutenant, missing the rams' horn badge of the Warlady's personal staff; and yet it was Sandrine, Sandrine as he had first known her and loved her.

"Put this on!" She shoved the bundle at him. "We're taken. I'll be just a prisoner, but if they capture you and know you're an electromancer…"

"…they'll put me on a courier ship for Calpurnia so their scientists can take me apart," Jauffre finished grimly. "I am a weapon." He remembered this all too well, knowing what awaited him if he was captured. The Calpurnians didn't have electromancers. They wanted his skills. They wanted his genes. He looked down at the bundle in his hands, the plain brown shipsuit of support services. It would mark him as a cook or technician, the lowest enlisted rank.

Sandrine nodded. "Go!" Her eyes said other things, but there was no time. They were out of time.

"Yes," he said, and she turned and sprinted back around the corner, the sizzle of her energy flail igniting as she rounded the corner.

He ducked into the nearest compartment, changing into the brown shipsuit with shaking hands, stuffing his own clothes into a drawer and locking it with an electronic click. Nobody would look there for days. The shipsuit was too big, but he doubted anyone would notice that.

Jauffre stepped out into the corridor again. Almost immediately there was a shout. "You there! Hold and get your hands up!"

A boarding party. Jauffre raised his empty hands over his head, his head down. "I'm unarmed," he said. "I surrender."

They surrounded him briefly, checking for weapons. He kept his hands up and his posture slumped. Jauffre was very good at being submissive. Prodded with a boarding pike, he winced but made no hostile move. He was herded into the lower decks mess, a large room with little in it but tables and benches, and twelve or so support staff in the brown shipsuits. The Calpurnians pushed him in and closed the door. Jauffre heard the electronic lock engage and smiled. He looked up.

Some of the others were pacing, some sitting on the benches. One man sported a bruise across his face and a woman was nursing a swelling wrist, but no one seemed seriously injured. He knew all their faces, if not their names. They'd all been on *Golden Promise* for nearly a year since it had been converted from merchanter to light warship. One of them, a big tech named Mackie, straightened up from where he stood with one foot up on a bench. "If it isn't the electromancer."

"Will you hush?" one of the women said. "We don't need extra attention."

"He's an electromancer," another tech said.

"He's our electromancer," Mackie said quellingly. "So what do you know that we don't?"

Jauffre shrugged. "They've captured the command center. The ship is taken."

"We're screwed," someone said. "They'll keep us on a hulk somewhere until the war ends."

The door opened again. The Calpurnians shoved in two more techs, landing crew from their insignia. The door closed behind them. "The captain's dead," one of them said. "I heard a Calpurnian say so. The command crew are mostly badly wounded or dead. They've got some junior officers in the brig."

"Right," the woman who had told them to hush said. "That's done it." Mostly dead. A few junior officers. Sandrine hadn't been in the command center. She'd said that it was taken before he saw her. Jauffre took a deep breath. She'd be one of the officers in the brig then.

"Have you heard what it's like on the outsystem hulks?" a man said. "That's near a death sentence there."

"Well, what do you suggest we do?" one of the techs demanded. "We're locked in here with no weapons."

"They'll put a prize crew in charge," Mackie said. "The ship's in good shape. They won't scuttle *Promise*. Not too many people in a prize crew."

The tech got in his face, still in fighting mode with nowhere for it to go. "And we're still locked in here!"

"Not for ten seconds longer than we want to be," Jauffre said. Everyone looked at him. "I can get that lock open faster than I can say it."

"Two guards in the hall," the woman with the swollen wrist said. "With energy pikes."

"Better and better," Jauffre said. "I'll overload the pikes and you rush them."

One of the techs looked incredulous. The woman with the swollen wrist nodded slowly. "I've seen what an electromancer can do. If you can overload the pikes, there's fourteen of us on two of them."

"We just pile into them," Mackie said.

"And then what?" someone asked.

"We free the junior officers and retake the ship," Jauffre said. Everyone looked at him. Jauffre tilted his chin up. "Do you want to spend years on a hulk? I certainly don't want to be the Calpurnians' prisoner. I know *Golden Promise*'s systems inside out. I can open the armory. I can shut down weapons systems or open them. I can't get into the main core without an interface, but I can shut doors and lock them in wherever they are. That's simple. Just put it on a breach protocol at any tech station and then open doors wherever we need to."

Mackie nodded. "So most of them are trapped in whatever compartments they happen to be in when you tell *Promise* there's a hull breach. Then we get to the brig, take on any small groups we run into on the way, and let the officers and flight crew out."

"There's a small arms station in the guard room just aft of the brig," one of the women said. She looked at Jauffre. "Can you open it?"

"If I can get to it, I can open it."

"Then we're on," one of the landing crew said.

"Not right away," Mackie said. "Give them a couple of hours to get comfortable. Let the prize crew settle in and give whichever ship is grappling us time to get off. Three or four hours, maybe."

"That sounds good," Jauffre said. "We wait."

And so they did. Four hours seemed forever, the clock in the mess slowly changing. Nobody came in. Nobody checked on them. Presumably there were more important things for the prize crew to be doing. This far inboard there were no hull sounds to tell them anything. There was no engine vibration to suggest a large burn, and the steering thrusters couldn't be felt here, the woman with the bad wrist said. They waited. And waited.

Jauffre leaned back against the wall and closed his eyes. The net of wiring inside the wall surrounded him in familiar comfort, *Golden Promise*'s capillaries carrying its lifeblood of electricity. He could follow their bright tracks even without an interface. And beyond, in the corridor, two separate electrical sources, the heavy batteries that powered a pair of energy pikes. He'd never tried precisely this, not overloading them without touching them, for all his assertion he could. And yet they were basic heavy batteries. He wasn't trying to manipulate something fine and complex. He felt for the potential energy, the electricity they stored. There. All it required was to release it suddenly. The pikes would overload. Yes, just there, like squeezing a fruit too tightly.

"Castal-Edo?" Mackie touched his shoulder tentatively. "You asleep? It's time."

Jauffre opened his eyes. "I'm ready." They were watching him. He hoped they saw the kind of man with cold enough blood to sleep between battles. He got to his feet with a little smile. "Let's do it. I'll get the lock. Then wait until you hear noise in the corridor before you attack. It will take me a moment to overload the pikes."

The woman with the swollen wrist nodded. "We've got it."

"Then." Jauffre passed his hand over the lock, closing one circuit in *Golden Promise*'s familiar systems. The lock disengaged. He closed his eyes, reaching for the battery packs. Just a squeeze and then... the sound of swearing in the hall, a clatter as though a pike had been dropped. He could feel the charge, feel just how to shape it.

An explosion. The door opened, crew piling out. Jauffre opened his eyes, still seeing spots from the overload he'd created. He leaned against the wall for a moment, listening to the sounds of the bloody melee in the corridor. Then he followed.

One of the guards was dead, smeared bloody streaks against the wall, his head at an unnatural angle. The other was shrieking on the floor, hands blackened with burns where she'd been holding the pike when it overloaded. Mackie lifted a foot to kick her in the head.

"She's out of the fight," Jauffre said, pulling at his arm. "Come on. We don't have time to waste." He felt his stomach roil, and dragged Mackie down the corridor. "We have to move fast. Where's the nearest tech station?"

"Down here," someone said, opening a panel a section down to show a set of connections and cables.

"Perfect," Jauffre said. He reached in, resting his fingers on the incoming cables. Yes, that one. Sensors were supposed to automatically trigger breach procedures. So easy to simply send a pulse along the waiting line.

Claxons blared again, lights flicking red. Thumps sounded throughout the ship as sections sealed, vacuum doors shutting in every space, corridors and ventilation shafts alike. The entire ship went to alert. Even now the command center doors were sealing. The prize crew wouldn't override—not yet. They'd wait to find out if the hull breach was real. It was all too plausible that there had been damage in the fight that hadn't seemed severe, but only now after a few hours had resulted in a blown-out compartment. Just for good measure, Jauffre sent two more signals from disparate directions. It would take them quite a while to sort it out, and probably need a suited visual inspection before they decided it was a false alarm.

"We're trapped, too!" one of the techs said. "The corridor's sealed at the junction."

"Except that you have the electromancer who can open it," Jauffre said. He strode down the hall to the closed door, shutting his eyes as he put his hand to the wall. And there, just beneath the skin, the tracery of wires…. The door slid open.

Something hit him hard in the hip, knocking him to his knees in an explosion of pain. "Get them!" one of the women yelled, and the crew members surged past him, swarming over the two Calpurnians who had been in the hall. The one who'd hit him with the butt of the pike went down under the wave. The woman with the bad wrist reached down with the other hand, and he grasped it, still gasping. "You all right?"

"Yes," Jauffre said. "Didn't see that coming." He could stand. It was a bruise, just a shock, not real injury.

"You can't sense people?"

"Not really," Jauffre said. "Not easily, in a place full of people like a ship. Your electrical signature is so much less than *Golden Promise*'s."

"Interesting," she said.

He put his head to the side, taking a deep breath. "You're not afraid of me?"

"You're on our side," she said simply.

"There is that."

She put her fist to her forehead in greeting. "Crew First Class Celie Vogel. And you're Castal-Edo."

"Call me Jauffre," he said. It was good to feel he had one firm friend in this at least.

"Jauffre then." She looked down the corridor. "They're stuck at the next juncture."

"Time for the human door opener," he said with a smile.

"I suppose that's one use for electromancers," Vogel said.

They stormed their way aft and down one deck, encountering little resistance. Few Calpurnians had been in the corridors when the doors had sealed. When they passed compartments where people were banging on doors and shouting, they simply ignored them. If they were locked in, they could stay there.

The corridor leading to the brig was empty, the heavy doors sealed. Jauffre put his hand to the wall in a now-familiar pattern, the doors opening back. Four barred cells were beyond in darkness except for the fitfully blinking emergency lights. Sandrine was in the first one, staring at him like he was an apparition. Whatever clever line he'd meant to say died on his lips. "We're retaking the ship," he said. He put his hand on the lockplate. "I'll get you out of there."

Her eyes swept shut for a moment, a secret smile on the bow of her lips. Then the door opened and she pushed it wide. "Crew of the *Golden Promise*, form up. Castal-Edo, get the rest of the cells open and then the guard station. I take it there is no hull breach?"

"No, Over-Lieutenant," Mackie said, drawing himself up. "It's a ruse."

"Excellent. Are all compartments sealed?"

"All except the ones we cleared on our way here," Vogel said.

Jauffre was opening the other cells. Three young Black Guards. One of the engineering crewchiefs with his arm in a sling. Two weapons officers, both junior to Sandrine. They thanked him as he opened the doors.

Sandrine was counting. "We've got enough for a command crew. Adai-Fersson, you stay back and don't engage with that broken arm. Vogel, is it? You too. Everyone else will draw weapons from the guard station."

"Over-Lieutenant, ours are here," one of the young Black Guards said. He passed her a sword in its long black scabbard, her own blade, necessary for controlling electromancers. Also useful in a melee and faster than an energy flail.

"Good," Sandrine said. She settled it on her hip.

The way to the command center was clear. Jauffre opened each bulkhead door and closed it behind them so that no one could follow if they were able to get out of some compartment. They stopped outside the command center doors. Inside, they could hear movement and voices.

Sandrine pulled them back around the corner. "All right," she said, "There are going to be at least eight of them, maybe ten. All of them are going to be heavily armed. We know they won't have projectile weapons since they were a boarding party, and you never inflict projectile damage on a starship you plan to take as a prize."

Mackie grinned. "Less mess to clear up."

"Less chance of depressurizing the entire thing and killing yourself," Sandrine said quellingly. "We have two boarding pikes, five energy flails, and two blades."

"And me," Jauffre said.

"You have to open the door. And as soon as you do, we rush them." Sandrine looked around at each of them. "Saka-Green, I want you to go straight for the communications station with your flail. Take out whoever is there before they can contact anyone outside the ship. Havel-Jumei, I want you to go for navigations."

The pair of Black Guards nodded. Each of them was armed with an energy flail. Sandrine next told off each of the weapons officers, assigning them a station to take; one was armed with a flail, the other with his own blade. "Mackie and Sammedi, you've got the pikes. Go wherever the resistance is toughest since you've got the reach on everyone. I'm going for the officer of the watch." She looked at Jauffre. "You stay off to the side of the door after you open it until we've cleaned them up. You're not a melee fighter."

Jauffre nodded his agreement, as did the others. It was interesting being part of the team. Any relief he felt at not being part of the general rush was deeply buried. He was not, after all, a soldier. Most of the support staff hadn't been issued weapons or asked to charge either.

"Ready?" There were agreements all around. "Remember," Sandrine said, "Communications first. And by Blessed Khreesos, don't hit the interface boards with energy weapons!"

They approached the door again, Jauffre off to the right, Sandrine in the center, everyone ready to go. Silently, she nodded to

Jauffre, her blade in her hand. He bent his head, opening his hand against the door panel. There were the fibers, tiny sparks traveling through the network of wires and circuits, the web that fed into the command center as thick as the starfield looking toward galactic center. Nevertheless, there was the same familiar junction.

A tiny push. The doors slid open. "For Morrigan!" Sandrine screamed, and they charged in, weapons crackling.

There weren't ten Calpurnians. There were fourteen. Sandrine vaulted over the captain's acceleration couch, bringing her blade down in a sweep with her entire weight behind it, nearly severing the officer of the watch's arm. Blood fountained. A Calpurnian threw up her pike, catching the blow Mackie tried to land on it, struggling face to face, the pikes shorting and shooting sparks at their contact.

So much power. So much energy. It was like being dipped in ice water, like being drunk on frozen wine. It called, it sang, it crackled around him, making his skin prickle. The lights flickered alarmingly, screens shifting. Sparks and a sudden poof of smoke rose where someone had indeed hit a control board with an energy weapon. The melee heaved and flowed in the strobing light like a sickening fantasy of dancing.

A Calpurnian lifted an energy flail bristling with power, each strand reaching out like tentacles. It would hit Sandrine full on as she straightened up, blade in hand, full across the shoulder and left side of her face.

Jauffre didn't think. It was there, every bit of it, every wild electron. He pulled it out of the air, out of the wires, out of the weapons, lightning sparking from his hands as though he were one of the electrified strands itself, catching the Calpurnian with the move half completed, his own flail sparking suddenly bright as the tentacles twisted, each limned in purple light.

Sandrine's return thrust caught the Calpurnian in the chest. Lightning crackled on Jauffre's fingertips, and he threw it at the nearest Calpurnian, the current crawling across her, knocking her to the floor.

Someone shouted. He could hardly hear above the scream of power. His hair stood on end, his hands wreathed in twisting current. He threw again. It arced across the room, taking down another Calpurnian, and then the rush was gone and he staggered back against the wall, trying to breathe, to bring his racing heart back into rhythm.

Vogel was at his elbow. "You okay?" Jauffre nodded. He couldn't quite speak yet.

"Get that board locked down!" Sandrine was yelling orders at someone. He saw her slide into the bloody captain's chair, pulling the command arm across her, her fingers dancing on the interface. The screens around the command center shifted, an exterior view of their location from three forward cameras.

"Shit," Mackie said. He had two prisoners, their weapons dropped before them and their hands up. "We're in the middle of the Calpurnian fleet!"

At least five capital ships surrounded them. *Golden Promise* progressed slowly between two warships, while two more were ahead and one behind, a pinnace and a tender off to the side. It was a beautiful sight, one certain to inspire awe in any spacer who witnessed it, especially from in the middle of it on a prize ship.

Already the comm channel was chiming, someone asking if there was a problem aboard *Golden Promise*. Sandrine pulled her headset on and keyed open the channel. "We've got a hull breach warning. It looks like something blew from damage earlier. We can stay under way, but we're endeavoring to isolate the problem. In the meantime, we're under full breach procedures." She attempted a clipped Calpurnian accent.

"Understood, *Golden Promise*," a voice said. "Keep us advised. And put Tarsnia on the line, if you please."

Sandrine's eyes widened slightly, her accent shaking into broad parody. "My apologies. Tarsnia is investigating the breach. We'll report shortly." She cut the line.

"That sounded like the villain in a bad vid," Jauffre said, and Sandrine gave him a dirty look.

The weapons officer who had seated himself just forward of her twisted around on his couch. "Now what? They'll buy that for about a minute."

Sandrine's mouth hardened. "Get me three windows for microjumps in-system, starting now. I don't care what our destination is. Adai-Fersson, main engines are online. Prepare for jump. Sound the chime now." She looked at the weapons officer. "Clear all missile tubes. You will fire on my order."

He spun back around, leaning back and looking up as he pulled the interface down, jump straps still unfastened. "Clearing tubes, Captain."

Sandrine pulled one of the straps across her one-handed, the other still on the board. "Helm control to this station."

"You have helm control," Adai-Fersson replied. "Main engines are cycling. Ready in six."

"First jump window in twenty-seven seconds," the navigations officer shouted across the din.

"We'll take it," Sandrine said. "Jauffre, sit down."

There weren't enough couches. He sat down on the floor next to Vogel, his back against the carpeted wall beneath the screens. There was nothing else to brace against.

"Weapons, fire on eight. Main engine burn on eleven. Counting down. Two, three, four, five, six, seven…"

Eight was drowned out by the deep rumble of all four of *Golden Promise*'s missile tubes firing at once, four 500s streaking away, two to each side toward the Calpurnians who rode alongside at point blank range.

At the same time Sandrine put the helm over, *Golden Promise* diving beneath their plane like a kraken diving for the depths, the main engine going to full two seconds later. "Five seconds to jump!" Sandrine said. Jauffre flattened his hands against the floor. The screens went white, then darkened again compensating for the visible light burst.

"All four missiles are a hit!" the weapons officer said. "I've got an atmosphere plume from one of the capital ships!" A cheer ran around the command center of *Golden Promise*.

"On my mark!" Sandrine shouted. "Punch the jump!"

There was sudden distortion, the pressure shoving him hard against the bulkhead. Suspended. Pinned, like a moth in a display case. Ten heartbeats, and then they were through, the screens resetting. Morrigan rose in three-quarter eclipse, a sliver of light side bright against the circle of the dark side, inside the Belt. Home.

Sandrine was confirmed as acting captain. *Golden Promise* had a good cleaning at Orbital Three, prisoners taken off to hold for eventual exchange. Jauffre stayed with the ship. Sandrine wasn't technically his guard anymore but continued to keep her old quarters, guarding the electromancer. Very prudent, Jauffre thought. Who could fault her diligence—and if her nights were spent rather closer to her electromancer than regulations required, anyone would assume she could do as she wished: Captain's privilege. After all, he wasn't truly crew.

Not that you'd know that from the rest of the crew. As far as they were concerned, he was their electromancer. No one was afraid to have him at table in the mess, and more often than not he was part of the jokes, part of the conversations. No one flinched when he reached for a dish. No one sneered or speculated. It was... different.

He said so to Sandrine, late one night when they lay together worn out from sex and talking. "I wish it could always be this way," she said. And then, practically, "It would be better for the fleet, too."

"We'd serve better if we served willingly," he said.

She brushed her hand across his brow, that too-knowing expression on her face. "I want nothing from you that isn't willing."

"I know that," he said, and if he might have said more, he drowned it in kissing her shoulder, finding every sweet nerve ending.

A hundred days. A hundred and nine. Armistice. The Calpurnian Fleet jumped outsystem, and diplomats went to work. No more blood would spill like wine in the void. The Lady of the Void had drunk her fill.

The Guard contingent that came aboard wore full dress uniforms, and they saluted the ship's company. "Captain Dal-Vesta, the Archegos Dariah, Warlady of Morrigan, sends you her compliments. She requests that you report as soon as is convenient. You are to join her personal staff."

"I am deeply honored," Sandrine said, making a bow with her fist on her forehead as though she bowed to the Warlady herself. Her eyes met Jauffre's, and he nodded, his heart as full of pride as pain.

The College had finished the Lustration of the Dignitaries. Leonie kept her face serene. It had not taken nearly as long as she'd hoped with the speeches and the choir cut out, but there was at last no way to drag the Lustration out any longer.

"Let us move to the nominations," the Speaker intoned. "Aware of the gravity of our work, in full reverence for the task before us, does anyone have a candidate of standing and impeccable character they wish this College to consider?"

The Hierarch rose from his seat again. "Colleagues, there is one among us whose worthiness is undeniable. I nominate Sister

Leonie, Hierophant of the Sema." Leonie had been warned by Serene Tomas. She remained perfectly still in her chair.

"I give this nomination my approbation," the First of the Academy of Practical Sciences said ponderously. He was nearly ninety and had been new to his position when she had come to the Sema thirty-five years ago, a child of seven with extraordinary talent as a Dreamer given her modest progenitors.

"I give this nomination my approbation as well," said the hawk-faced First of the Academy of Social Engineers.

"And I as well," added Serene Tomas, "on behalf of the Order of the Golden Lady."

For a moment Leonie froze. She could not pretend she had never dreamed of being Archegos. Attending on Dariah all these years, the ambition of ascending to the Seat of Khreesos had certainly occurred to her. The changes she could make, the wrongs she could right with a word, rather than through careful diplomacy and subterfuge! And yet, even if it were not a deadly trap, she was no warrior. An administrator, a politician, adept at managing personalities and logistics—without false modesty, there was none better. But to fight a war against Calpurnia? For a moment, just a moment, she could put that aside. She could be Warlady. All she had to do was nod.

It was a deadly trap. She would go into the interface and she would die like Dariah. The only reason that the Hierarch, who had never liked Dariah's reforms, would nominate her was if he knew. Was he the hand behind the assassination? There was one way to be sure.

Leonie smiled. Serenely, she rose to her feet, holding her hands away from her side like a supplicant in gratitude. "My dear colleagues, Worthies all, I am speechless with the honor you give me. I can imagine no greater joy than the confidence you repose in me." Her eyes swept over them. Yes, the Hierarch looked happy, his mouth twisted just a little in what might be a smirk. "However," she continued, "I am not the right person to lead Morrigan in this time of military crisis. The times call for a warrior. Therefore, I must decline the nomination, and instead nominate a man whom I have admired for many years and whose leadership is well known to all of you: Luca Weld-Savarin, Hierarch of the Black Guard."

If she had been an irreverent acolyte, she would have said he nearly fell out of his chair. He was ambitious. He would like to be Warlord, but was too high-handed, too close to contemptuous of some of the College. Under normal circumstances, he would not be nominated, at least not until Dariah's preferred candidates were dead or discredited. He was the last person Leonie could be expected to nominate.

He looked stunned, and for just a moment afraid. Now Leonie knew for certain. He had set the trap. He had killed Dariah. She saw it in his face. He was terrified of going into the interface, and only she and the assassin knew it was trapped.

An approbation or two rang out, seconds to Leonie's nomination. She met the Hierarch's eyes as he stood up. He knew that she knew. Leonie nodded graciously, a dagger in her smile. She would kill him for what he had done to Dariah and she would make it his own hand which wielded the weapon. She saw the anger in his face as he saw the choice before him. Ambition would die before he would. "You do me too much honor," the Hierarch said gruffly. "I decline the nomination." He sat back down.

Uproar followed. The most prominent faction leaders had both just declined. The College broke into wild argument. Who, then? A physician? A priest? Aides ran about carrying verbal messages from one to another since screens were forbidden on the floor. The Hierarch was conferring with a Black Guard very quietly. An accessory? An interesting question. Leonie lifted her chin as she put a quiet call through Windfollower into the Sema's systems. *Follow and track the aide when she leaves the chamber*, Leonie ordered. *Record and observe*. It would not work, of course, if the aide entered private areas that were not part of the security net, but Leonie would know where she went at least.

Arguments raged. Nobody had enough of a following. Those who preferred Leonie were leaderless. Those who might have supported the Hierarch were shocked by his refusal. The Speaker fruitlessly called for order. At least, Leonie thought, it was taking time. She stood to request a recess for lunch, early but surely welcome given the number of private conversations people wanted to have.

The Nautarch beat her to her feet. "This is ridiculous," he said in a carrying tone better suited to battle than temples. "I nominate the Somatophylax Sandrine Dal-Vesta. She's a Black Guard, a warrior, and the Warlady's chosen at the same time."

"I give my approbation," the Hierarch said, though for very different reasons. He'd be happy to see Sandrine dead.

"And I as well," Serene Tomas said with something like relief. "The Archegos Dariah thought highly of her."

"And she is a Black Guard," someone else said. "She was a ship's captain in the war despite not being Fleet. Surely as military matters go…"

"…the Warlady's Somatophylax is fully qualified," the First of the College of Trauma Physicians said. "She has my approbation as well."

Leonie felt the strands slipping through her fingers. If Sandrine went into the interface…. "The Somatophylax isn't here," Leonie said. "She can neither accept nor decline the nomination."

"Well, where is she?" the Nautarch demanded. "Surely this gathering is worthy of her attention!"

"She is on the trail of the Warlady's killer," Leonie said. "I have every confidence she will shortly produce evidence of who is behind the assassination." She did not look at the Hierarch. She didn't need to.

Uproar again. This time it was Serene Tomas who cut through the babble. "Speaker," he asked politely but loudly, "is it required that the candidate be present to be voted upon? I seem to recall that Warlord Argheeros III was elected though he was aboard ship and in another system at the time."

"We did things very differently then," Leonie said. "That was in the era immediately following Khreesos's death, when the leadership remained for several generations within one family."

"Still, there is precedent," someone said.

The Hierarch smirked. He might be presumed to be doing so because he wanted a fellow Black Guard enthroned. "I move that we call the vote on the Somatophylax Sandrine Dal-Vesta and if she later chooses to decline, she may do so. When she returns she can enter the interface immediately and then present her findings in this investigation."

Already some were looking at Leonie curiously. Why was she speaking against her friend when she had already declined the nomination? And yet she still had no proof. There was no accusation against the Hierarch she could make. Surely Sandrine would have enough sense to stay out of the interface. That was why she'd taken Castal-Edo with her. As long as nobody else was nominated and accepted, there would be no candidate in the interface until Sandrine returned and could tell them what had happened. It would, at least, preclude the nomination of some entirely innocent person who would go into the interface and be killed.

"With great pleasure, I give my approbation to the Somatophylax's nomination," Leonie said.

Chapter Seven

Sandrine looked down at Jauffre in the chair. "Jauffre? Jauffre?" And yet he didn't answer. He didn't stir. Only the slow movement of his breaths continued, the movement of his eyes as though he dreamed. Twenty minutes. Twenty-five. She knew better than to pull his fingers out of the interface. She'd known since she was a child that you never wake a Dreamer. She'd pulled her father's fingers free once when she was small, watching him stagger about disoriented and retching before he finally collapsed on the floor. "Never," he said, "ever pull a Dreamer out of interface. You could cause brain damage."

Sandrine paced around the chamber again, the mosaics bright beneath her feet. Half an hour. All right, she couldn't pull him out of the interface, and indeed there was no reason to think he was in distress. But what if something were wrong? Who knew with an interface this old, this unused? What if he couldn't get out as he was supposed to be able to? The interface was trapped. They both knew that. What if he couldn't interrupt the cycle?

Sandrine stopped next to him. His hair fell back from his forehead, more gray than dark now, the lines of his face relaxed as though he slept. She had known every line once, but there were new ones now. She had known every expression. What if he didn't wake?

And suddenly it was unbearable, seeing him lying there unmoving, waiting for a power surge that would burn him as it had Dariah....

She lay down on the right-hand chair, gritting her teeth. "Khreesos, help me," she said, and slid her fingers into the interface pad.

Sandrine stood beneath the starry sky. No, it was the starred ceiling of the Antechamber to the Presence, deep in the heart of the Sema. For a moment she shook her head, confused. How was she back in the Sema?

"If you will come this way, Captain?" A young man of the Black Guard was waiting deferentially halfway across the floor. Perhaps he thought her awe-struck by the beauty of the temple.

"Yes, of course," Sandrine said quickly. For a moment it seemed odd to her to wear the uniform of a captain again. Surely….

And off to the side was the Cella, the private chambers of the Archegos. The Black Guard opened the door and stood back. "Your Graciousness, here is Captain Dal-Vesta."

The Warlady Dariah turned, and Sandrine went to one knee as was proper, her fist to her forehead. Then she ventured a glance up. The Warlady was still in late middle age, her close-braided hair beneath the circlet with the gilded rams' horns over a black floor-length tunic of deceptively simple material, its wide borders embroidered with gold. "Rise, Captain Dal-Vesta. I have looked forward to meeting you." She nodded to the young Guard, who departed.

"You do me too much honor, My Lady Archegos," Sandrine said, returning to her feet. Something was wrong. There was something she should remember. And yet what could it be? She stood before the Warlady for the first time, fresh-come from *Golden Promise*.

The Warlady put her head to the side. "You are probably wondering why. Walk with me, Captain."

"Of course." Sandrine fell in deferentially beside her. Together they went through a side door that led to one of the balconies surrounding the temple courtyard. Lights blazed below, illuminating each gilded terrace.

The Warlady paused, looking out over the brightness below. Above, the stars were faded in their light. She looked up. "We must prepare for war," she said quietly.

"Graciousness, the Calpurnians are defeated," Sandrine said. "They have withdrawn from our system entirely, abandoning even the bases on the outer planets that they had captured."

"For now." The Warlady gave her a sharp, sideways glance. "I understand that you have a talent for tactics. Now we will see if you have a talent for strategy. It is not enough to think one move ahead. You must think of the endgame while you are still in the beginning."

"I don't understand," Sandrine said.

"The Calpurnians have based their entire economy on expansion. They are not self-sufficient. They require a steady stream of goods and material flowing in at prices to their advantage. It makes them rich, yes. But it means that there must always be more—more markets, more demand, more people who require or believe they need the things that Calpurnia supplies. They are not stable. Their systems do not balance. It doesn't matter which of the Altissimi is on top. All of them face the same problem: how do you ensure constant growth? How do you feed a creature that will never be satisfied?"

Sandrine frowned. "That is a very different way of thinking."

"Yes." The Warlady's posture was straight. She did not lean on the railing at all. "The environment of our world has shaped us. On Morrigan, everything must be sustainable. Nothing can be wasted. We have wealth, but every time we have allowed powerful families to amass too much, they have fallen in their time. We have tried our hand at conquest and we were mighty. But since Khreesos's time we have stayed behind our starry walls, rich, brilliant with art and science, untouchable."

Sandrine shifted from one foot to the other. The Warlady smiled. "And you are too well-disciplined to argue with me. You must learn to argue with me. You are thinking, *we are too hidebound, too unwilling to change our ways*, and you are right." Her smile broadened as Sandrine blinked. "We withdraw too much. We do not aid our allies with force as we once did. We send money and hope that suffices. We allow Calpurnia to expand and if it is not into our territories, we shrug. When they destroy Menaechman passenger vessels we respond with a strongly worded protest."

"And what should we do?" Sandrine asked cautiously.

"One by one, their rivals fall. Inanna is reduced to nothing, and perhaps that was a just war. It was nearly two hundred years ago. Then the Freyar were pushed back until nothing remains of their sphere except Freya Prime. Then in the next generation it was Lono hosting their garrisons and calling them overlord. They have tried us, and through the courage and blood of people like you, they have withdrawn. They bit on a nut and found it too tough. But they will be back." The Warlady shook her head. "Now they test Menaechmi. They will find it easy pickings. The Cities of the Coast will have no choice but to enter into alliances not to their advantage or find their cities reduced to rubble, a client state of Calpurnia. And when they have finished with that, they will be back for us." She spread her hands. "Who shall we turn to then? Our potential allies will have already fallen."

"Freya?" Sandrine suggested.

The Warlady nodded. "Willing, but with little to offer at this point." She looked across the bright courtyard to the lights of Holyrood far below. "We are the last and strongest of the old powers. We must prepare."

Sandrine took a deep breath. It was true. She knew it in her bones. And of course the Warlady knew it, Khreesos's heir with his genius in the Presence which touched her. The Warlady watched her face. "So," she said, "what would you do, Captain Dal-Vesta?"

Fortune favors the bold. "I would unleash the electromancers."

One of the Warlady's eyebrows rose. "Before they were closely kept, every high-caste line had their own electromancers, their own kindred who did their will. How do you guard against those who can stop your heart with a hand to your wrist, or who can make a weapon of every electronic thing that you touch? It was an endless round of assassinations and murders and destruction of innocent people before we took them all under guardianship and limited who might request their genes so that we kept a core but did not allow powerful families to raise their own. You would change that?"

"Graciousness," Sandrine said carefully, "that was a long time ago. We cannot match the Calpurnians in numbers or in ships. Yes, ours are as good, but as you say they have many more. We cannot match them in wealth when they may draw upon many worlds and we but one, rich as it is. What we have that they do not is our blood. They do not have and cannot use the technologies that our ancestors created. They do not have our blood-gifts, refined for generations. They do not have Dreamers. They do not have electromancers. That is our only advantage. We must use it."

"And will they not turn on us?"

Sandrine chose her words carefully. "That was not my experience in the war, no. Certainly there are those who have been ill-used. Far too many. One is too many. But they are not different from us. They want the same things we want—to sit in a tea shop with friends, to take lovers as they please, to form an Academy for study, and to have good work and respect. If we give them those things, they will be loyal."

The Warlady smiled. "And you have told me what you want. But is that true of them? All of them?"

"No doubt some will do wrong. There are always people who do wrong. And when they do, we take them under guardianship.

But we do not lock them away because someday they may do something wrong. In all other ways, we do not punish potential crime."

"We wait until there is an actual victim," the Warlady said dryly.

"Yes," Sandrine replied. "I may commit a murder. And I may not. To lock me up for something I have not yet chosen to do is unjust."

"Because you do not believe blood is destiny." Sandrine blinked, and the Warlady paced a little way along the balcony, Sandrine following her as she tried to assemble her thoughts. "We are taught," the Warlady said, "that genes are immutable. Our identities are written in the double helix, and we go through our lives like faithful little machines, following the spiral path they lay before us. Even when it seems we choose, we do no more than reveal a hidden recessive. We have always been the thing we are revealed to be. We are fatalists. What will be, will be." She turned. "And how will we stand against Calpurnia when we don't believe that we can write our own destinies?"

"I believe," Sandrine said. "I choose. And maybe I choose wrongly, but if so, it is my own fault, not a fault in my chromosomes."

The Warlady nodded slowly. "You will serve as my personal aide from this day and hour. And I will consider your suggestion. It cannot be done in one swoop. Perhaps first there should be electromancers at court. Three, perhaps, who will be my guests and demonstrate their skills recently honed in battle against the Calpurnians. People will twitch, but they cannot gainsay me in that."

"Can anyone gainsay you?" Sandrine asked. "You are the Archegos!"

"Do not be so shocked!" The Warlady laughed. "I owe my power as much to the College as the Presence. I am no Calpurnian Autarch. I am duly elected by my peers, and I must answer to them.

I can't simply make a declaration and change the world. If enough of them do not accept change, it will not last, and the backlash will make things worse than before."

Sandrine nodded slowly, and the Warlady patted her wrist. "Learn, Captain Dal-Vesta. Lend me your passion and your loyalty, and we will see where our choices lead us."

"I am your true servant," Sandrine said, and bent her head in respect.

It was deep winter when the electromancers came, the roofs and courtyards limned with a dusting of snow. Jauffre Castal-Edo was one of them, of course. He was very precise, very beautiful in his embroidered surplice of midnight brocade, his demonstration of powers clear and masterful. He was well-spoken in his deference, as she knew he would be. When the Archegos asked, before all the court, what the electromancers desired, he replied that they wished to visit from tower to tower, or send representatives periodically to some common place, that like any other Academy they might share their knowledge to the betterment of wisdom and Morrigan alike.

"I see no harm in this request," the Warlady said. "And much good. You do not ask for anything for yourself?"

"Only that my presence continue to please Your Graciousness," Jauffre said with a bow. On the other side of the room, Leonie was watching him closely, and Sandrine saw her smile at that.

"Then perhaps we might allow a convocation of electromancers under my protection here, one year from this day," the Warlady said. "I shall look forward to your presentations on that date, Castal-Edo."

Afterwards they fell into one another in Sandrine's luxurious little room as though a thousand years had passed instead of not quite one. *My heart, my light, my pride, my beauty, my treasure*—there were enough endearments to carry them until morning.

"My beloved," Sandrine said, half-asleep at last, his face against her hair, "I wish that morning never came."

"That's why we live on the dark side of the planet," Jauffre said, and slept.

In the fifth year she was made Somatophylax. She wore the Warlady's horns on her breast and all of the Guard save the Hierarch obeyed her. She traveled to Menaechmi on the Warlady's behalf. She traveled to Lono, a young electromancer named Augie accompanying her. She had not dared ask for Jauffre. Once a year was enough.

It made her careless. Her aide walked in on them, and he, loyal and honest before, lied for her and kept her secret. She was not diminished in Over-Lieutenant Danzi-Jean's eyes, but she was in her own. Her aide lied for her while she cavorted with a lover. In the cool light of false dawn, the lights coming up to illuminate the courtyard outside in an imitation of the diurnal cycle, she took a last bowl of tea by the window with him. "We can't do this, Jauffre."

"I know." His voice was regretful, not surprised.

"It jeopardizes everything we are doing," Sandrine said. "I am the Somatophylax. If we are exposed, it is no longer about what is right and fair for all electromancers, or even about what is best for Morrigan. It is simply my own personal vice which I wish to indulge."

His hands were long and elegant, a caress on the fragile porcelain of the tea bowl. "So much good, so much change…. My youngest apprentice is allowed to talk to her mother on the net rather than just scream for her until she goes to sleep. It's not her fault she manifested at five. But now she can see her mother's face every other day. Her mother can read to her rather than just mourn her as one dead."

Sandrine blinked. She had never asked. "How old were you, Jauffre?"

"Nine," he said. He swirled the tea around the bowl. "My fathers wanted a child, and one was prepared to be the progenitor. They were told they could have the donation of a female electromancer who would carry the baby and give it to them. I don't expect they considered whether or not she would want to give her child away; she would have preferred to keep it—me—but it wasn't up to her. They were told that the chances were less than ten percent that I would be an electromancer. It seemed good odds to them." He lifted dark eyes to her. "I was wanted and loved by two fathers who cherished me. They were broken when I manifested."

"Ah, Jauffre."

He shook his head. "You're right, of course. This matters so much to so many. We are making progress. We can't jeopardize that." He took a deep breath. "We have had something lovely and we need to move on. We know this can't last. It's time to let it go."

"Yes," Sandrine said, and her voice didn't shake at all.

He put the bowl carefully down on the edge of the table and stood up, her lean, elegant, sweet and dangerous lover. "I should go."

"You should." She didn't stand. If she did, one of them would reach out. One of them would touch. And then all resolution would be dust.

"Goodbye, Sandrine." She looked down, but she saw his hand hesitate. She didn't move. She heard him take another breath. He drew on his brocade surplice, and she watched him settle it properly on his shoulders, fastening the frogs across his chest.

"Goodbye, Jauffre," she said, and heard the door close behind him.

The next year when the electromancers came to Holyrood, she was on Orbital Three launching a new capital ship in the Warlady's name.

The darkness around him was absolute. There was not even the tiny spark of an electrical wire from which he could kindle a tiny point of light. Jauffre reached out, his knuckles scraping on the stone wall, and he knew where he was. He was in the solitary confinement cell at New Houston. He heard his breath coming loud in the darkness. No, he would not panic. He had been here before. He had been here before more than once. He pressed his hand against the wall. You could push and push against these walls and nothing would happen. They were solid stone. There was no net of wiring within them.

Dark, because any electricity can be a tool to an electromancer. Eight paces long and six wide. A soft bedroll that had no metal parts. Nothing affixed to walls or ceiling that one could hang oneself from. A mechanical lock. Breathe. New Houston. He'd spent sixty-two days in this cell once for defiance. For coming to Eulalia's defense. Pointless. He'd been locked up and done her no good.

The rage boiled around him, cracking like static electricity, but there was nothing to gather it from. And even if he gathered it, even if he threw it, stone walls did not yield. There was no way out. Jauffre took a deep breath. He knew what to do—pushups and poetry had gotten him through before. He'd outlasted the trap.

Trap. Jauffre frowned. The interface was trapped. His body lay in a chair in the tomb of Khreesos. "This isn't real," he said. It was a conjuring of horror from his own mind, a memory of being trapped turned into a cage.

In which case, he had the key. Jauffre stepped back to the middle of the room, raising his arms to the side as though he greeted an imaginary audience, the lead actor making the old-fashioned customary demurral at the end of the play. "If we spirits have incurred/your displeasure and thus interred/our hopes, our loves, our very sight/beneath the shadows of your night/I pray that you will consider/that you did but dream here/and these your fancies that appear/to vanish in the morning's light."

A dream that fades into a better dream. Jauffre raised his hands, shaping the darkness, shaping the interface where it touched his mind. *I will step forward*, he thought, *into a better dream*. The door of the cell was suddenly limned with light. He put his hand on it and walked through.

Jauffre threaded his way through the reception, the click of his boot heels loud on the polished marble floor. They were his favorite boots and rather new, gold mesh spotted with gold in a raindrop pattern with a gilt toe and heel. His trousers were midnight and gold brocade, a long midnight coat over it. He was, he felt, adequately holding his own for the electromancers. After all, everyone at the party was gorgeously dressed. The worthies of Holyrood were in attendance for the Archegos's pleasure, high-caste, scholars, Dreamers, and members of various academies all wearing their colors in a dizzying, brilliant show of plumage. Among them, the deep indigo of the Guard stood out.

Jauffre made his way between two women in scarlet and stopped. This reception was four years ago. He had been at Holyrood for the last convocation that had been held there, before the Warlady permanently established the annual convocation at Seville, allowing a small gathering of electromancers under her patronage. The last three had been held there. Another dream, then, but a better one.

And there—the balcony doors were open to the night, fountains playing beyond, their falling drops illuminated in a muted rainbow. Sandrine stood beside the doors, her dark uniform unrelieved except for the Warlady's rams' horns embroidered on her tight-fitted jacket. In a moment he was going to speak with her. They would stand in a very public place exchanging pleasantries. She would ask him how he had been and he would ask her how her life was. They would say little and never touch.

What if he didn't? He turned around. The Warlady stood behind him. "Walk with me, electromancer," she said.

Jauffre bowed deeply. "Of course, Your Graciousness." They passed among the guests unremarked. No one followed. They simply went out into the garden. The Warlady sat down on a carved bench and motioned for him to do the same. "I have been eager to speak with you," she said.

"This didn't happen," Jauffre said. "Who are you really?"

"Who are you really?" the Warlady asked. Her gray eyes were very keen.

"Jauffre Castal-Edo," he said. He thought he understood. "I'm here to unbind the trap that holds you, Agathos Daimon."

The Warlady smiled. Or her likeness smiled. "Clever man. I would be glad of your help. But I do not know that you can undo it until it is sprung."

Jauffre frowned. "Wasn't it already sprung? Forgive me, but wasn't it sprung when it killed you? Killed her, I mean? The Warlady Dariah?"

"Partially," she said. Her eyes roved his face, and it occurred to Jauffre that the Warlady's eyes had been dark, not this piercing pale gray. "The second part of the trap will trigger when an elected candidate steps into the interface. This way not only will the Warlady be dead, but the candidate most likely to follow in her footsteps will be as well. There are two murders. The first has happened. The second has not. The candidate is already in the interface. As soon as the vote is taken, she will be in grave danger."

"Sister Leonie?"

"Sandrine." The Warlady put out her hand, holding to his arm.

"Why is she in the interface? I told her…" Jauffre began.

"To be patient?" the Warlady asked. "Have you ever known Sandrine to be patient? Of course she went in when she feared for you."

"She's no Dreamer. If she were, she wouldn't have needed me to begin with."

The Warlady smiled. "And I expect you will need her before this is done." She looked up, around the walls which seemed to be the Sema, but were really those of the tomb. "I have some autonomy here, backed up in systems which are only tenuously connected to the Sema. But if Sandrine tries, even accidentally, to access the Sema, the trap will close."

Jauffre nodded. "How do I defuse this trap? If it can be set, it can be undone."

"You are very certain of your skills."

"Yes." Jauffre looked up at the falling droplets of the fountain. "Why this trip through my memories?"

"I wanted to know who you were," the Warlady said. "And now that I know, I believe you can untangle the trap. It will not be easy, but I trust that you can read the metaphors. They are no less deadly for being virtual dangers."

"I understand," Jauffre said. He was silent a moment, watching the fountain and thinking. "Can you get me to her so that we share the same virtual perception?"

"Simple enough." The Warlady raised her head, looking toward the balcony doors. "This is a memory you share. Tell me what happened."

"Very little," Jauffre said. "I attended the reception. Sandrine and I spoke for a few minutes. It was…difficult."

"To want so much and have so little." The Warlady's voice was quiet.

"Yes," Jauffre said. "And then I talked to other people. I made myself personable to various worthies. That's all that happened."

He looked at whatever the Warlady truly was. "I didn't speak to the Warlady."

The Warlady nodded slowly. "Then walk away from me and back into your memory. We will speak again, Jauffre Castal-Edo, when you have undone the trap."

Jauffre got up, looking back only when he reached the door. The bench behind him was empty, the fountain falling unheeded. He threaded his way through the crowd. It was warm from so many people, even with the doors open to the garden, scarlet walls with gilded molding a bright backdrop for a brilliant crowd. He stopped and bowed to a worthy wearing the black, swept-wing mask of one of the Greater Gifts.

And there was Sandrine again by the doors, just as he remembered. He made his way through the crowd to her, her eyes never leaving him the entire time. Wordlessly, they stepped out onto the balcony, standing four feet apart. "Jauffre," she said.

"How have you been, Sandrine?" he asked.

"Busy. I have a very busy schedule. And you?"

He had been destroyed by the sound of her voice, the hesitation over ordinary words, so that it had been hard to find his own. What had he said? "Busy also," Jauffre said. "I have my apprentices. And I'm working on a theoretical problem. Is it possible to glitch the guidance systems of a missile without touching it? We have an old guidance system and we're practicing turning it off from across the room." Jauffre smiled, sitting down on the edge of the balcony as he remembered doing. He hadn't been sure four years ago that it worked. How far along in the experiment had they been, exactly? "So it will be useful if the Calpurnians ever fire non-moving missiles at us from across a room."

Sandrine laughed. She sat down on the balcony too. Their hands were two feet apart on the rail. Hers moved closer. She glanced down at it, a little frown on her face. "That sounds like a very useful experiment."

"I hope that it will be." What had he said next? Something about teaching? The conversation stood out less clearly in his memory than her expressions. He could have said anything. It was her face he savored. His hand moved a little closer, casually, as though just shifting on the rail.

"You're teaching?" she prompted. It was like an actor reminding a colleague of a dropped line.

"Yes, teaching," Jauffre said. He looked at her, but Sandrine's eyes were on their hands. Hers had moved a little closer. Was this a memory, or did they but perform the drama of their lives? What if he did something he knew he hadn't done? Very deliberately, Jauffre put his hand over hers, warm skin and cold stone railing, his fingers sliding like silk along hers.

Sandrine looked at him, her eyes wide. "This didn't happen!" she said. "We didn't touch."

They both moved at once. He held her tight, his face against her hair, ducking to kiss her with all the passion he'd held in check four years ago, as though a scene was made right, a story given a different and better ending. But this wasn't a story. It was real. The jeopardy was real. Jauffre lifted his head, still holding tight to her. "Sandrine, you shouldn't be here. You shouldn't be in the interface."

"I was worried about you."

"There's a second trap. It will trigger when a candidate goes into the Sema's interface." He held her back at arm's length, his hands on her lower arms. "Sandrine, they're taking a vote on you right now. The Presence warned me. If you're elected, the moment you touch the Sema's interface, the trap will snap."

"They can't elect me! I'm not even there!" she protested.

"Don't ask me how they're justifying it. But they're electing you Warlady right now. And we have to reach the Presence and free it without touching the Sema's systems." Jauffre shook his head. "It wouldn't have tripped for me because no matter what happened at the College, I wouldn't be a candidate. But you are.

It's your life on the line if I fail."

Sandrine took a deep breath. "Warlady."

"If you live so long." He clutched her arms tightly, as though they stood in a whirling stream and he was afraid of being swept away.

Her hands were tight on his arms too, but her voice was perfectly calm. "All right. What do we do? You're the expert. I'll follow your lead."

"It's going to take both of us, the Presence said." Jauffre found her calmness steadying. "We need to think it through. The Presence said that there were systems that were not physically part of the Sema's system, and that's how it could speak to me. We're inside a memory core that's here in the building. We have to stay in this memory bank and not touch anything in the Sema. We have to find the broken connections and restore them so that the Presence again has full control of the system. Then it can turn the trap off. Right now it's locked out of the Sema's systems and can only stay in the memory here."

"Which the person who planted the attack didn't know about," Sandrine said grimly. "They meant to destroy the Presence itself."

"But they didn't succeed because it's backed up on the systems here," Jauffre finished. "What I saw when I went in before, the visual metaphor, was the ruined temple in the desert. I couldn't reach it no matter how I tried and I couldn't manipulate my surroundings the way I just did here. I think the ruined temple is a visualization of the Presence's systems."

She looked thoughtful. "The ruined temple as a metaphor makes sense. But it's also part of Khreesos's story." Jauffre spread his hands and she continued. "There's a story that gets a bare mention in one of the memoirs and a bunch of legends in the apocrypha about Khreesos going on a trek through the desert on the Light Side to find an ancient oracle to fulfill a prophecy. I don't know whether this ever happened or not, or whether he went to the Light Side for some other reason, but I can guess now why the story isn't in the canon."

"Because in the story he's an electromancer," Jauffre said.

"There isn't any other explanation for the events of the story if you believe them," Sandrine said. "When the histories were edited to justify locking up the electromancers centuries later, that story had to become fantasy. It had to be purged from the Sema's memory core."

"But surely various Archegoi have touched the Core over the years. Surely they've touched this memory core."

"And said nothing about it," Sandrine said grimly. "First because they were the ones who did it and then…." She shook her head. "No wonder Dariah wanted me to question. No wonder she listened to me about the electromancers. She already knew. But she knew that she didn't have anything like the support she would need to undo what had been done. She could have made a legal change, but cultural change comes harder."

"And without that, it would all fall apart. As it would if she moved too fast." Jauffre looked toward the remembered reception still playing itself out beyond the balcony. "Even so, someone killed her for it."

Sandrine nodded. "So now we have a motive but not a killer."

"You can find the killer when you're Warlady," Jauffre said. "Right now we need to reconnect the Presence to the Sema's systems without you triggering the trap."

"So we find the ruined temple." She frowned. "Which is essentially an un-updated version of the Presence, one where the older files haven't been purged. That's suggesting the Presence is an AI."

Now was not the time for Sandrine to have a crisis of faith. "Or is indeed an upload of the Warlord Khreesos into the Core. However the Presence began, we need to help it." Jauffre held her hands tightly. "I can't build a purely imaginary version of the Light Side. I've never been there. And I don't know the story of

Khreesos's journey. You're going to have to picture this. I'm going to have to build on your memories."

"And then?" she asked. "How does this work?"

"Everything we see around us here," he gestured to the balcony, the garden, reception inside, "is based on our memory of a real place and moment. They're tiny electrical impulses traveling back and forth between our brains in the interface chairs and the memory core. What I can do is alter those electrical impulses through will."

"How do you know what language to use?"

Jauffre smiled. "My love, it's not the language. It's the commands. If you enter them correctly, the interface will translate them into the correct code."

Sandrine put her head to the side. "I'm not quite seeing it."

"You don't need to. Just visualize the Light Side. You can imagine it based on memory and story. You are with Khreesos and you've gone into the desert to look for an ancient oracle." He bent his head to hers, forehead to forehead. "Close your eyes. Make the picture as real as you can."

Beyond the rim of light over the world, there was the Light Side, beyond the seas that washed endlessly against the walls of Sea Easting. It was there in Sandrine's mind. He'd done this with another electromancer, linking together, but never with someone who wasn't even a Dreamer. But there was a bridge. There was the physical link between the two chairs' interfaces.

Words are intention. Words are command. He found it in the words of a poet dead three hundred years, saying them aloud while holding tight to Sandrine. "We will make love be our bridge/over oceans lit with stars/and I will clasp your hands/between these ensilvered bars./My love, give me your kiss." She tilted her head up, their mouths meeting. Will. Will to carry them, will to take him where Sandrine dreamed, every ounce of his being focused on the words, the kiss, a bridge to carry them.

And the world around them changed.

CHAPTER EIGHT

Sandrine stood in the desert, the intense heat of the Light Side pouring down on her. Her arms were tight around Jauffre, her boots sunk to the ankles in sand. She was still wearing the dress uniform she'd worn to the reception all those years ago, and wished for a moment that while they were changing the world they could have changed into more practical clothing for a desert trek. Jauffre was in that gorgeous night-sky blue with the gold embroidery and what had to be the sexiest and most impractical boots she'd ever seen.

He saw her looking at his feet. "I could take them off and go barefoot," he suggested.

"You most certainly can't," Sandrine said. "The sand is sixty degrees. You'll flay the skin off the bottoms of your feet if you try to walk on it barefooted."

"I will now that you've said it," he replied.

"Can't I say that we're wearing something more reasonable?" Her dark, high-collared jacket was already stifling. "If I'm creating the scene, surely I can wear whatever I want."

"Be my guest," Jauffre said, letting go of her. "Now you're thinking like a Dreamer."

Sandrine closed her eyes. She could hear the wind whispering over the sand, sculpting it into a thousand fantastic shapes, like waves of a still ocean. *Khreesos came this way*, she thought. *I am with*

Khreesos, walking into the desert to find the Oracle. This is how they came. This is how they looked, what they wore. She built the picture from animations she'd seen, from words she'd read. *I am with Khreesos.*

"Oh, very nice," Jauffre said.

Sandrine opened her eyes. He was wearing a long robe of white gauze, every bit of it treated to reflect the light, including the deep hood that shaded his face, a cold pack against his back to maintain proper body core temperature. Sandrine looked down at her own light, flexible-treaded boots, the reflective white gauze robe worn over the pleated short skirt of the Warlord's army, projectile rifle at her back, ammunition slung across her chest plate ornamented with gilded rams' horns. She smiled.

"You look like a picture I've seen somewhere," Jauffre said.

"This chest plate is in the Academy at Fulgar Landing," Sandrine said. "It belonged to Argheeros I, who is my seventeen-times grandfather five ways. I've always liked it."

"It looks good on you." Jauffre grinned.

"Yes. Well. We should get going." Sandrine climbed the nearest dune, Jauffre following.

"Where are we going?" he asked.

"West," she said, "Toward a dry river course on a plain of salt. The river course had a deep trench which was always shaded and cool. And there lived a hermit who tended the Shrine to the Scorpion Mother, to Lady Death." She'd always loved this story, and Jauffre was an attentive audience.

"I thought nobody lived on the Light Side."

"There aren't any settlements, now or then. But there are a few people who live on the outskirts even if nobody could survive long in the deep desert. Remember, I grew up at a research station in the Transition Zone. There were weather stations further out. Most of them were remote-access, but every astronomical year someone would come out and maintain them when Morrigan was at its farthest point from the sun, about every two regular years."

"Have you ever wondered," Jauffre asked as he hauled himself up a dune, "why we have three hundred and sixty-five day years, with each day being twenty-four hours, when it has no correlation with planetary time?"

"We don't rotate," Sandrine said. "So why should those who came here change their measurements from ship's time? We don't have time zones or days and nights, so why not stick with whatever they were used to?"

Jauffre looked intrigued. "So our time measurements are the original ones, preserved by the Core and by our ancestors, having no need to change?"

"That's what I think." Sandrine shrugged. "You know what a pain it is going back and forth between Calpurnian Standard, the Lonoi and Menaechman really complicated systems and ours. If everybody is used to something as basic as how you tell time, why change it unless there's a compelling reason to? They had reasons to. We didn't."

"That actually makes sense," Jauffre allowed. He stopped at the top of the dune, looking down across the trough to the next one even higher. "So why did Khreesos want to find this hermit?"

She smiled. Jauffre was always fascinated by a story. "There was a prophecy that the Calpurnians could be defeated by the one blessed by the Scorpion Mother. Khreesos was having a lot of political problems getting the other great families to agree to attack Calpurnia preemptively under his command. Remember, he wasn't Warlord yet. There was no planetary Warlord. There were a dozen great families and their territories. So he decided to take a few dedicated followers and go into the desert, find the Shrine, and get the Scorpion Mother's pronouncement that he was the prophesied leader. The story is that they traveled twenty days in the desert…"

"…please not," Jauffre said.

"…and then they found the Shrine along its abandoned riverbed. The Keeper of the Shrine came forth and asked Khreesos why he had come, and he said that he had come to get her blessing." Sandrine slogged into the trough and started up the next slope. "She said that she would give her blessing when he made it rain in the desert. So Khreesos reached heavenward and opened the skies." Sandrine stopped on the slope, waiting for them to both catch their breath.

"And that was why you knew the story had to be stricken from the narrative."

Sandrine nodded. "When I first read the story, it didn't make sense. It seemed utterly imaginary. How could anyone do that? But in the tomb, when we saw that Khreesos was an electromancer, it all fit."

Jauffre nodded slowly. "The clouds," he said. "The evaporation from the Eastern Sea, carried by the jet stream around the planet. When cold fronts pass over superheated desert, the rising and descending air separates positive and negative charges. If you discharge it, you can trigger the rain. That's how lightning works."

"And so the hermit, the Scorpion Mother's oracle, would only give her blessing as Warlord to an electromancer who was strong enough to manipulate currents at ten kilometers." Sandrine smiled triumphantly. "If you can't do it at ten kilometers straight up, you can't do it at ten kilometers to incoming in a space battle!"

"That's close range for a missile or a starship," Jauffre said. "I've been able to close or open circuits at twenty with a lot of practice, but ten is about the limit I'm absolutely confident with. And that's just to close a circuit to glitch a guidance system, not actually throw lightning. If Khreesos did it, he was an extraordinary electromancer."

"We know he was extraordinary," Sandrine said. "Anyway, the story says he brought the rain and the oracle gave him the Scorpion Mother's blessing. He went back and rallied the remaining houses to his banner and led the fleet against Calpurnia. That part is history."

"Then I suppose we'd better keep walking," Jauffre said.

Leonie looked around the assembled worthies who were just regaining their seats after the lunch recess, talking—and politicking, of course. Elen slipped up beside her, bending low next to her ear. "Mother, I didn't think I should put this on the system."

Leonie kept her face impassive, as though she were hearing about some minor catering problem. "Tell me."

"The surveillance systems tracked the Hierarch to the lower guardpost. He talked to the watch captain, who seemed agitated in the video. They talked for eight minutes. Then the Hierarch left again. The watch captain made a comm call to one of the systems technicians."

"On duty in the Core?" Leonie asked quietly.

Elen shook her head. "Not today. They were last on duty in the Core two days ago." Leonie's mouth pursed. "The day before the Archegos...."

"Don't say that aloud here, Elen," Leonie said. She looked around, meeting her daughter's eyes. "Take the Sema's guards. Detain the technician and the watch captain as quietly as you can."

Elen tensed. "You want me to detain a watch captain of the Black Guard? Quietly? He's not going to just do what I tell him."

"I'm sure you can manage," Leonie said. She dropped her voice even lower. "Even if all you do is put him in a room he can't leave or communicate from. Do you understand?" Elen could do it, but it would be dangerous, and she didn't dare suggest how. However, losing the Hierarch's conspirators would be worse. She had to prove his guilt, and she'd bet that at least some of his subordinates in this plan didn't know what they had done.

"Yes, Mother."

"I can't loan you Windfollower. Its absence will be noticed."

Elen nodded. She glanced up as the Speaker began to call the

College to order. "I'll do it. Don't worry." She made her way off quickly between the chairs as the convocation quieted.

Don't worry. As if that were possible, Leonie thought.

"Worthies," the Speaker began, "All impediments now dismissed, I call the vote on the Lady Somatophylax Sandrine Dal-Vesta. Shall she be presented to Blessed Khreesos as our candidate to succeed to his chair as Archegos, the Warlady of Morrigan? You shall each express a vote of yes, no, or abstain when your name is called. I shall call the roll now."

Leonie glanced across the firelit hall, the flames in the gas-fed braziers casting strange and archaic shadows on glittering detail on robes, on the headdress Greater Gift of the First of Social Engineers. There was no more time to stall, short of a dramatic medical emergency. But if she suddenly fell on the floor in a dead faint, she would be attended to and the vote would continue. *Sandrine*, she thought, *be careful. Oh my friend, be careful!*

"Hierophant of the Sema, how do you vote for Sandrine Dal-Vesta?" the Speaker asked.

Leonie got to her feet, composing her robes. "Worthy Speaker, my vote is yes."

Sandrine stood on top of a sand dune, looking out across what seemed to be the Western Desert, rather than an analog in the system. Which of course meant there was no actual way to know how far they had left to go; all distances were imaginary. Above, massive white thunderclouds gathered, swept eastward on the jet stream, tops flattening and blurring in the high winds aloft. She saw Jauffre glance up. Whatever the weather was doing, he felt it. But of course it wasn't real weather. The weather was an analogy in this place. "Jauffre, what's going on?"

He frowned, slogging up the dune toward her. "Gathering

storm. It's a metaphor for something. That we're getting closer? That it's getting more dangerous? I don't know yet." Suddenly, his eyes widened. "Sandrine! Watch out!"

There was a sound behind her, sand shifting and pouring, and suddenly over the lip of the dune came an enormous scorpion. It was fully as long in the body as she was tall, its barbed and poisoned tail held aloft, its legs skittering. It barreled toward her. Jauffre shouted something she didn't catch.

Sandrine unslung the archaic projectile rifle from her back. This was her dream, so it was loaded. She lifted it to her shoulder, leaning into its length as she brought the sights to bear on the scorpion's head. Its tail rose. She shot twice, chitin flying as her bullets hit. The scorpion collapsed in a mass of ruddy legs in in front of her.

Jauffre clambered up the dune to stand beside her. He looked completely unnerved. "What in the name of Blessed Khreesos was that?"

"A giant scorpion," Sandrine said. The rifle was warm in her hands. "They're in the story. But we could have done without them." She patted the rifle. "Khreesos's soldiers fended them off with projectile rifles. I can take care of it."

"Well, I'm so pleased to hear that," Jauffre said. "All those legs."

"It's the poisoned tail you have to watch," Sandrine said. "Once it sticks its needle in you, you die in minutes."

"Metaphorically, one hopes." A shadow suddenly crossed his face. "Unless it's another warning. We'd better hurry."

"We're almost there," Sandrine said, willing it to be true. "They were nearly to the oracle when they met the giant scorpions." Very deliberately, she turned, looking down the dune, looking for the dry riverbed.

It was there. There was the gorge, there the baking white salt flats. Her breath caught. Beyond was the ruined temple, broken walls sticking up from the sea of sand. In the center, a column of pale light stood where the Presence was in the Sema. It was beautiful and unnerving at once, the center of the maze, the road to the Core. "The Presence," Sandrine said.

"Sandrine, we have a problem," Jauffre said, his voice scaling up.

She spun around. Charging toward them over the dunes beneath the streaming sky were fifty or more of the giant scorpions. Their chittering was louder that the first roll of thunder overhead. They were all coming straight for her.

"They've taken the vote!" Jauffre said, "The trap is sprung!"

"Run!" Sandrine shouted, grabbing his arm and propelling him down the side of the dune with her. "Run for the temple!" She had twenty shots. Twenty shots for fifty scorpions was impossible, and there would be more. There would be as many as the trap required. Hundreds. "Run!"

The sand dragged at them, and she hauled Jauffre along. They were gaining. "Keep going!" Sandrine shouted. She unslung the rifle again, standing coolly to line up the shot. There was the sharp crack and the nearest one tumbled, fouling the one behind it. Second shot, and the one behind it stumbled, injured, falling onto its body. Third shot, and the one behind that went down, clear ichor staining the sand. Then she turned and ran after Jauffre.

He had reached the edge of the salt flats, where sand gave way to a packed crust that crunched beneath his feet. Just beyond, the first broken walls stood knee-high. Overhead, the clouds roiled.

The broken walls were a maze. Waist-high, chest-high, round and round in senseless patterns, the Presence always out of reach, always around another turn, and behind the scorpions pursued. Sandrine stopped at a defensible corner, shooting two more, their falling bodies blocking the way behind them. "That should slow them down," she said with satisfaction.

"Not for long," Jauffre said. One of the scorpions mounted the wall, charging over it rather than following the turns as they did.

Sandrine swore, aiming again. She caught it in the head and

it fell from the wall, tumbling to rest just at Jauffre's feet, its tail trembling. "Go!" she shouted. "Keep going!"

Another turn, another twist, the walls higher than they could see over, the chittering louder behind them. Or in front of them. They came out of a twist into what might be the ruins of a larger room, roofless and open to the sky, the floor scoured with sand. Scorpions poured in through another entrance across from them, impossibly many, ten or more.

Sandrine stopped. "Back to back!" she said, putting herself at Jauffre's back so they faced in both directions. "Just like in a boarding party." Eleven shots, and then she'd draw her blade. They'd done this before, storming aboard a Calpurnian ship.

"Of course, my love." He raised his hands with a little smile, drawing from the ambient, and then the scorpions were upon them.

Lining it up, two shots that told, and then two to take the third scorpion down. She felt Jauffre step, and they rotated together, his hands wreathed in indigo glowing tendrils of current. Cool wind hit her. The storm front was upon them. The purple clouds boiled. The scorpions were too close. She drew her blade, slashing at a scorpion who threw itself toward her, lightning limning the steel as it bit. The scorpion fell back, black burns in its shell. The wind whipped around them.

She knew the story. Even in the heat of combat, she knew the story. "Jauffre!" Sandrine shouted over the rising wind. "Bring the rain!" She felt his left shoulder move against her back, and she turned as he raised his hand, white robe flapping in the cyclone, a gesture of command, lightning racing upward from his palm to split open the sky.

There was a deafening crack, her vision momentarily going white the same instant as the rapport, and Sandrine reeled, trying not to fall in sudden blindness. And the rain came down. Water, thick as a from a shower, drenching, lashing, completely and suddenly soaking, drove her to her knees, still blinking.

Jauffre was at her side. "Sandrine? Are you all right?" He was kneeling in the suddenly wet sand beside her, his arm over her back as though it would shelter her.

"I think so," she said. The spots were receding. Her vision was clearing. "The scorpions?"

"Gone," Jauffre said. He helped her to her feet. The rain poured down her face, the robe plastered to her arms, her blade still in her hand. "But that's not."

She shoved her soaking hair out of her face, looking where he did. Where the glowing column of the Presence had stood, there stood a man. He was not tall, shorter than Sandrine by a little bit, wearing the same antique armor that she did, his hair dry despite the downpour, watching her with keen gray eyes.

"Blessed Khreesos," she said, and went to her knees again. Behind her, Jauffre did the same.

"Stand up, Sandrine Dal-Vesta," he said. "And your electromancer." His eyes flicked to Jauffre and back again.

She got to her feet. "We have done as you asked and found our way here. What must we do to break this trap?"

"You already have, Warlady."

Sandrine closed her eyes. "I am not worthy. Sister Leonie…"

"You were always meant to be the candidate," Khreesos said gently, and she opened her eyes. "Dariah intended for you to follow her. Just not…" he hesitated, "…so soon."

Sandrine searched his face. "You were with her when she died."

"I was." He met her eyes. "It was quick. She did not suffer."

Sandrine looked away, out across the desert cloaked in pouring rain, rivulets flowing already on the sand. "I am glad to hear that."

"She intended for you to be her successor. Dariah knew that you could do what was needed." Khreesos leaned on one of the broken pillars casually, as a man will on some piece of furniture in his home.

"I have always thought that Leonie would be the next Warlady," Sandrine said. "I was prepared to support her."

Khreesos shook his head. "I think well of Leonie and always have, but she is no warrior. This war with Calpurnia has been coming, and it was inevitable that it would begin, sooner or later. We need a starship commander, not a Dreamer." He tilted his head, and his voice was kind. "You may think that you would be more if you were a Dreamer, or if you had my own gift as an electromancer, but consider that if you had been a Dreamer you would never have served in the Fleet, and if you were an electromancer in this time you would have been locked in a tower. Sandrine Dal-Vesta, you are exactly who you are supposed to be."

Sandrine blinked, her eyes unexpectedly filling. No one would notice with the rain. "You are the Warlady," he said. "Right now. You are the elected candidate. You have gone into the interface. And you have been accepted."

"By the Presence," Jauffre said behind her. "If you don't mind me asking, are you actually Blessed Khreesos?"

"Jauffre!" Sandrine spun around. "This is not the time!"

Fortunately, the Presence did not seem offended. He leaned against the pillar, considering. "I don't know," he said. "Not the answer you wanted, Castal-Edo? But it is the truth. It seems to me that I am. I remember my life, my victories and defeats, my loves. It seems to me that these things happened to me. But did they really, or am I simply programmed from the same sources you have read?"

Sandrine blew out a breath. "But you know things that are not in the sources I read."

"True. There are many stories of me which are not in the sources you have read, stories which are no longer taught or are lost," Khreesos said. "History is continually manipulated and reinterpreted to suit the needs of the day, sometimes for good and sometimes for ill. I have no doubt you will tell my story in a different way again, and it will suit your needs and that of Morrigan."

"By saying again that you were an electromancer," Sandrine said.

"Just so." His gray eyes did not leave her face.

"What else has been taken out?" Jauffre asked curiously. "Just as an example."

"Jauffre!"

Khreesos's mouth twitched. "That I had two daughters by free breeding is one fine example, but not one I expect the Warlady will emphasize. She'll have enough on her hands with electromancy. That's enough work for the rest of her career."

"Providing my career isn't exceedingly short," Sandrine said. "I have to defeat the Calpurnian fleet." She raised her face to the rain. It was lessening somewhat. "Is it really possible to throw lightning from ship to ship?"

"Yes." Khreesos's answer was brief.

"It was done in your day?"

"And after, for quite a while." Khreesos shrugged. "Ships and missiles were simpler then, of course. Missiles still used liquid fuel, unstable and much more volatile than the solid fuel used today. Ships were slower and less maneuverable. We'd only been out of the Lost Era for two hundred years after the invention of the jump drive. But yes, I could throw lightning across the Void."

Sandrine nodded slowly. "If it could be done then, it can be done again."

"By your electromancer?" Blessed Khreesos looked Jauffre up and down, a smile playing about his lips. "I approve of your taste, great-niece."

"I beg your pardon?" Jauffre said. His incredulous expression was wonderful to behold.

She thought Khreesos might laugh. "We were not so modest in my era."

"As I recall, your personal life was exceedingly complicated," Sandrine said.

"And you don't know the half of it." There was that smile again.

It was very strange to almost feel him an old friend, daimon or disembodied soul or whatever he was. "Will you help us?"

"Of course," he said. "I will stand by you as I have stood by every Warlady or Warlord who has defended Morrigan, though you know that the Presence cannot reach as far as the orbital stations. When you engage the Calpurnian fleet, you will do so alone. And I have no doubt you will do well."

Sandrine frowned. He looked so alive, a man her own age with cares and worries. "Blessed Khreesos," she said hesitantly, "Do we put too much on you? To ask you to intervene in our troubles when you should have long since gone to your rest?"

He shook his head. "I chose this, remember? If Argheeros told it correctly, I wished to be placed into the Core. And if I was created for this purpose and am no more than an imagining of Khreesos, of course this is my choice." He looked out across the salt flat, now glittering with swirls of salt water in the rain. "I worry that I speak too much. That I give counsel when I should not. That was what the Hierarch thought: that I am a crutch to keep Morrigan from becoming what he would want it to be." He shrugged. "But if he were Archegos, his policies would bring Morrigan under Calpurnian rule in a year. I could not accept him as candidate, not if he were the only one. And perhaps that is putting my finger on the scales too much, but I can only do what I must."

"That sounds like you are an AI," Jauffre said.

"I don't know what I am, Castal-Edo," he said. "So you must believe what you wish."

Sandrine gave Jauffre a quelling look. "I believe you are the daimon of Blessed Khreesos, and that yours is the long task of guarding your people from your sacred Sema. So I believed, and so I believe even more so having met you."

"Stubborn as Argheeros," he said, and smiled again, that smile that must have lit his world. "And I have something for you which

I think will prove helpful. When you come out of the interface, you will know how to open one of the offering compartments. Take the Red Glove."

"What is it?" Jauffre asked.

"A Greater Gift that amplifies the powers of an electromancer. It was mine." He gave Jauffre a stern look that Sandrine did not believe for a moment, as though Jauffre were an unreliable apprentice. "So be careful with it." Jauffre had the good grace to look abashed.

"We will be careful," Sandrine promised. "And now?"

"Now you must return to Holyrood as quickly as you can. There is much to prepare before the Calpurnians arrive. I will meet you there."

"Of course," Sandrine said.

Khreesos looked at Jauffre. "Take her home, Castal-Edo."

"Yes, my good lord," Jauffre said, bowing like the loyal attendant in a play. He raised his hands as though addressing the audience, the last lines of the Death of Khreesos by Abi. "And, Worthies, our sorrows lay/upon his still-unweathered curls/honors greater than gold or pearls."

Sandrine closed her eyes and felt the world tilt once more.

Her hands rested on the arms of the old-fashioned couch, her fingers in the interface gel. "Sandrine?" It was Jauffre's voice, Jauffre leaning over her, a worried expression on his face.

"I'm here," she said. "I'm all right." She withdrew her fingers, the momentary disorientation fading. She had not spent a lot of time in deep interface because she was not a Dreamer.

He sat down on the edge of the couch beside her legs as she sat up, and she scooted forward and held him tight. This was real. This was not another dream. "You're safe," he said, and then again as though he hardly believed it, "You're safe."

"I'm Warlady." She pulled back, her hands still on his elbows, his arm across her lap.

"You are." There was that sweet and rueful smile, proud that she had excelled, sad that there was yet another thing to keep them apart. Well, she'd see about that.

"We need to find the Red Glove and get back to Holyrood," Sandrine said. "It's in one of the offering drawers. The third one from the left, I think." It was there in her mind as though it had been there all along. *As long as you are in the Presence, I can speak to you*, Khreesos said in her head. *But not beyond.* "I understand," Sandrine said aloud.

"Understand what?" Jauffre asked.

"I was talking to Khreesos."

He shook his head. "Now that will take some getting used to."

"He likes you." Sandrine swung her legs off the other side of the couch, getting to her feet. "And thinks you're hot."

Jauffre looked utterly confounded. "I'm glad. I suppose."

Sandrine laughed. Now it was done there was a kind of lightness, a relief. "He's a man, Jauffre. A man who's been a guardian spirit for a long time. He wasn't born a god, not like the Lady of the Void. He became more. And less." She went to the third offering drawer and opened the catch. It rolled out silently, as fresh as the day it was made. On white silk rested a left-hand gauntlet of red leather elaborately embroidered with gold thread, rams and lions and scrolling leaves. "The Red Glove," she said. Gently, she picked it up. "It feels like interfaces have been sewn into the layers of fabric."

"Like the ones over the ears on Windfollower," Jauffre said. "Interface pads in the fingers? Why is it left-handed?"

"So that he could use a blade with his right," Sandrine said. She knew that. She just knew, without effort, here in the Presence. She handed the glove to Jauffre. "This is for you."

Jauffre bowed to the dark column, taking it reverently from her. "Thank you, Blessed Khreesos. I will use it to serve your people."

"He's glad of that," Sandrine said. "But we need to go, Jauffre. The vote is over. We have to get back as quickly as we can." She looked at the dark column which held behind its impenetrable face whatever was left of Khreesos's body. "I will return. That I promise." And then, grabbing Jauffre's free hand, she led him from the chamber.

Chapter Nine

Worthies, I propose that we recess until Sandrine Dal-Vesta returns," Leonie said. She stood as she spoke. The vote had been taken. Sandrine had been elected with only seven votes against. She had stalled and stalled and stalled, tying things up with procedural argument after formality. Surely once Sandrine returned, she could contrive to allow her testimony before she went into the interface! Elen had detained the two witnesses, or so she hoped, but that would be pointless if Sandrine didn't return soon. She couldn't keep them long. How much longer could she keep this going?

The lights flickered. Everyone looked up, startled. Then they went out. Only the great braziers and troughs of fire remained, leaving the room in firelight as it must have been in ancient days.

"What has happened?" Serene Tomas said, his voice carrying. "Leonie?"

"I don't know," Leonie replied. The Sema's systems were showing a full restart, as though somehow the entire system were rebooting. That should not be possible. "Give me a moment." She put her hand to Windfollower.

Behind the open doors to the Sanctum, a light grew. It was bright white, and a man stepped out of it. He glowed, pale and bright against the darkness of the room, stepping through the doors. A hologram, Leonie realized, and then she knew him. She had seen him in the interface, had knelt before him. He was no taller than she, golden-haired, his old-fashioned breastplate with gilded rams' horns shining in the firelight, the Presence made manifest.

Most of the worthies were simply struck silent. Leonie threaded her way between them. "Blessed Khreesos," she said, sinking to her knees gracefully in front of him. "Agathos Daimon." Behind her, someone drew a breath. She heard the whisper run around the room. Generally no one but the Warlady or Warlord and the Hierophant saw this—the Presence personal, walking like a living man.

"Sister Leonie," he said. He stopped not far in front of her. His legs looked real, each golden hair on his calves outlined against the light behind.

Leonie lifted her head. "Why are you here, Worthy Lord? Why have you chosen to manifest in this way?"

"This isn't real," the Hierarch sputtered. "That's not Khreesos. That's not the Presence. What kind of trick is this, Leonie?"

"No trick at all," Khreesos said. "But why would you expect me not to be able to manifest if I wish, Luca? Could it be because you and your associates sabotaged the interface to the Presence itself, and in the process killed the Warlady Dariah?"

Leonie turned around, as did everyone else. The Hierarch was red with fury. "This is a trick. This is some gambit of the Hierophant's. It's a power grab."

"If I wanted to be Archegos, why didn't I simply accept the nomination?" Leonie asked. "I would have had the votes."

"Because you knew!" he snapped, and then stopped.

"Knew what?" Leonie asked with lethal coldness. "Knew that the Warlady Dariah had been murdered and that you had trapped the Presence? If I did it, then why would I have trapped the interface against myself?"

"You can say the same of me," the Hierarch said. He was breathing heavily.

Leonie stepped around the nearest worthy, Blessed Khreesos seeming to follow her. "But you did not expect to be the first-nominated candidate, did you? And when you were nominated, you had no choice but to refuse. If you were innocent, you would have accepted the nomination gladly."

"Pure speculation!"

"We will know if it is pure speculation," Leonie said sweetly, "when we ask for the testimony of your accomplices, Tavin Mirren-Wei and Jannine Weld-Colomb. They are both detained awaiting the pleasure of the Warlady. I understand that Mirren-Wei is professing his ignorance of the meaning of what he did and is eager to speak."

"There is no Warlady!" the Hierarch said.

"There most certainly is," Blessed Khreesos said conversationally. "This assembly voted for Sandrine Dal-Vesta. She entered the interface and I have accepted her."

"She hasn't been here!"

"Fortunately, there is more than one interface," Khreesos said. "Sandrine Dal-Vesta entered the Presence and restored the systems that you had locked. I am free. You would have destroyed me."

"You are not real!" the Hierarch shouted. "You are a hologram created by a computer. You are no more Khreesos than an actor playing him on the stage. Less, because he doesn't give pronouncements as though he were a god!" He looked around at the worthies assembled. "Do you give your allegiance to this imagining? Or are you men and women who would control your own destinies?"

"They give their allegiance to me." Leonie spun around. Sandrine stood at the far door, at the entrance to the antechamber, Castal-Edo just behind her. "They have elected me Warlady." Her voice carried. "Do you renounce the vote you have just taken, Worthies?" She strode forward, her heavy boots on the delicate marble floor, her blade at her side. She took off her gloves as she walked toward the Hierarch, unbending and unafraid. "I have found the killer of the Warlady Dariah, and it is you. I accuse you of murder."

"You have no proof of anything," he began. "This is politics."

"We have the pending testimony of your accomplices," Leonie said. "And of Blessed Khreesos himself."

"There is no..." he began.

Sandrine stopped a foot from him. "Listen, little man. I trusted you. I followed you. And you murdered Dariah in cold blood for power. You shame the Black Guard and the uniform we wear. You dishonor all we strive to represent—courage, sacrifice, and incorruptible honor. You are under arrest and will face a trial of your peers with all evidence presented." She raised her eyes to the Black Guards by the doors. "Arrest this man."

For a bare moment Leonie thought they hesitated. But then they saw Sandrine's eyes. The watch captain put his fist to his forehead. "Yes, Warlady," he said.

Sandrine turned back to the assembly. "I am grateful for the trust you have placed in me. We are better than this. Calpurnia is coming. We will meet them, and they will hear the roar of our missiles and they will be afraid! They will learn again that it is folly to come against Morrigan! Are you with me?"

"Yes!" shouted Serene Tomas, his sleeves flowing as he raised his hand.

"Yes, Warlady!" the Nautarch shouted. "We will make them pay!"

A cheer ran around the room, Castal-Edo in the midst of it like a bodyguard at her shoulder. Leonie touched the Sema's systems, everything running normally, subroutines soothing as quiet music, and brought the lights back up slowly. Blessed Khreesos faded away, a last secret smile for Leonie as the worthies crowded around Sandrine. It seemed that he was not needed after all.

Jauffre paused in front of the screen in the communications room, and the acolyte leaned over to help. "If you've never operated one of these before, this is what you press for the clear line out. Then you enter the code for your receiver. If you're not certain of the code, there's a search menu here."

"Thank you," Jauffre said. "I will need to look up some later. But I know this one."

"Let me know if you need help, Worthy," the acolyte said, and went back to his work on the other side of the room.

Sandrine was in back-to-back meetings with Fleet and Black Guards, but she'd given him a job: find as many electromancers as possible for assignment to the Fleet. This was actually easier said than done. To begin with, there were only about two hundred true electromancers divided between fourteen towers across Morrigan. Of those, fully half had talents that were unsuited to Fleet service. Of the remaining hundred, at least fifty were either children, too old for Fleet service, or not medically capable of it, like Eulalia. Add to that the necessity that they be willing—it was far too dangerous to take an electromancer on a starship who didn't want to be there—and it was a very small pool indeed.

Jauffre put in the code for Sea Easting. Best to do that one first. Of course it was answered by the Black Guard on watch, Enry, who Jauffre judged to have about the same amount of brain as a plant. He waited while Enry got the guard captain, and then explained what was going on. "The Warlady's staff will contact you with further details."

Darris nodded. He was a decade older than Jauffre, nearly at retirement, and happy for Sea Easting to be as pleasant a posting as possible. Four years ago he'd turned over the entire budget to Jauffre after Jauffre had provided him with an exhaustive document explaining every bit of clothing required for the growing apprentices complete with three possible ways of fulfilling each order with shopping links and pros and cons of each item. "I don't need to debate where you buy each kid socks," he'd said, handing the data card back to Jauffre. "Here's the total. Don't go over it. They can wear court dress and wet suits for all I care." Complete budgetary control of the electromancers' allowance left a considerable amount of latitude, and if that meant that there were small luxuries all around, it never exceeded the total. Now Darris looked grave. "So the Calpurnians are back."

"They are," Jauffre said. "And I'm seconded back to the Fleet. I'm asking for Boral and Arlaine."

"You think those experiments are going to work on the real thing?"

"I certainly hope so," Jauffre said. "The Fleet will send a flyer for them. Would you mind putting on whichever of them is closest so I can fill them in?" He made it sound like orders from above, which of course it wasn't, though he had no doubt he'd get a flyer if he needed one.

It was only a few moments before Boral came to the screen. Tall and lanky, his curly hair falling in his eyes, Boral always managed to look like he was about to apologize for something. When he learned to stand up straight and filled out a bit, he'd be a handsome young man. Jauffre had been telling him to stand up straight for ten years. Surely sooner or later it would have some effect. "Master Castal-Edo?"

"Boral, how is everything there? Is everyone all right?"

"Worried about you, mostly," Boral said. "You left suddenly and didn't call. We were starting to think...."

"I'm fine," Jauffre assured him. "But the world isn't. The Calpurnians are preparing to attack us again."

Boral's eyes widened. "Just like you said."

"Yes. I told you there would be the time to show what you've learned, what we've learned together, and now that time is here."

He kept his voice very even. "You and Arlaine will go aboard warships and guard their lives and your own, if you are willing."

"Are you joking?" Boral started laughing. "Of course we are! We're ready, Master. I'm more than ready. Do you know what ship? How big is it?"

"I don't know that yet," Jauffre said. "You'll be assigned where the Warlady commands. She wants one electromancer on every warship if we can do it. You and Arlaine will be on different ships, but I have no doubt you will both be needed."

"And where will you be?"

"I'll be aboard the flagship, *Immortal Fire*," Jauffre said. "Guarding the Warlady herself." He couldn't help letting the pride into his voice.

"Positive!" Boral said. "That's mega-pos, Master."

"The Fleet will send a flyer for you," Jauffre said. "Pack what you will need for a few days. And Boral? I have something I need you to do."

"Of course, Master." Boral straightened his shoulders.

"Tell Sai and Verla and Melisande that I'm fine and that I love them. We'll keep them safe, along with everyone else on Morrigan. Tell them I miss them and that I'll see them in a few days."

"Meli's been worried," Boral said. "She wondered if you were in trouble over…"

"I'm not in any kind of trouble," Jauffre assured him. "Give Meli a hug for me and tell her that if she were a little older, she'd be going with you and Arlaine. But she's only thirteen, and that's still too young. Just tell Sai and Verla that I love them and I'll see them soon."

"Yes, Master," Boral said. He'd actually drawn himself up.

Jauffre resisted the urge to tell him to pack clean socks. Surely he was old enough to think of that himself. "Then I'll talk to you once we're all aboard. Stay safe, Boral." He paused, trying not to smile. "And Boral? Have fun."

"You can count on that!" Boral grinned, and Jauffre cut the comm. If only every call would be so pleasant and every electromancer so willing. But then Boral and Arlaine were the only ones in Sea Easting even remotely capable of doing what was needed. Eulalia hadn't made any sense in twenty years, Taka was a pain in the nuts, and Farian was nearly ninety.

Jauffre took a deep breath. Might as well get the hardest ones over with. He put in the code for Heian and asked the guard on duty for Tessa.

She came to the screen immediately, a tall woman ten years Jauffre's junior, her high-collared green and gold tunic impeccable. "Yes?"

Jauffre outlined the situation as quickly and neutrally as possible, ending with, "That's why we need you, Tessa. You're one of the best. We need you on a warship to defend Morrigan."

She crossed her arms across her chest. "We need. You're a well-trained minion, aren't you?"

Perhaps an appeal to self-interest? "Don't you want to earn your freedom?" Jauffre asked as persuasively as he could.

"I have no interest in earning what ought to be mine by right," Tessa said. "We're kept in guardianship when we've done no wrong. We're treated like animals, bred for conformation and temper. You use your power to kiss their boots."

"Look, Tessa, I know we don't always see eye to eye—" Jauffre began.

"You mean I have complete contempt for collaborators." She shook her head. "If you think I have any interest in helping prop up a system that oppresses me, you're deluding yourself."

"Reform…"

"Reform means fancy clothes for you when we should talk revolution," she said. "We should take our freedom, not beg for it. There is no compromising about our rights as human beings."

"And there is no getting anything your way," Jauffre snapped.

"I am effectively getting things. You're doing nothing except talk and talk and talk. Oh, and getting other people punished. You occasionally accomplish that."

Tessa shook her head. "Future generations will despise you," she said flatly.

"If you're too pure to fight alongside me, I'll take my leave," Jauffre said.

He cut the comm, his fingers shaking on the board. He rubbed his hands against his trousers legs, grounding the electricity that crackled at his fingertips. It hadn't been much worse than he expected. If he was Sandrine's hidden vice, she was his much more public dirty secret. Everyone who'd been at the first four convocations had known he hadn't slept in the electromancers' shared room, and Briony had been at Heian then. She'd probably told every electromancer in the tower, and everyone gossiped like fury when they could. There were those who admired his political acumen and those who despised his methods. Fortunately, there were far more of the former.

Jauffre leaned back in the chair for a moment, pinching the bridge of his nose. Frankly none of that mattered right now. If the Calpurnians took Morrigan, all the electromancers would be prizes to take home and take apart, not to mention all their families and friends who would suffer under an occupation.

An antidote. He'd do Fulgar Landing next. He put in the code and explained himself to the Black Guard, then waited while the watch captain hunted up Rani Castal-Horst. Rani was seventy-two, with silver-white hair that Jauffre hoped he'd achieve rather than mundane gray. He might; they were related through the maternal line in the second degree. Her smile was genuine and warm. "Jauffre. This is unexpected. I heard that the Warlady had died and that the Somatophylax was the Warlady-Elect."

"That's all true," Jauffre said. "The Calpurnians are going to test us when they think we're weak."

Rani looked thoughtful. "So they need us."

"They do." Jauffre steepled his hands beneath his chin. "Can I get your most promising apprentice?"

"I'll do you one better, Jauffre. I'll bring two and come myself. We can't let these young folks have all the glory, can we?"

"Rani, I never…"

"I'm certainly capable of being aboard a starship," Rani said. "It's not as though you're asking for us to go wilderness hiking! Starships have nice, even floors, regular meals and soft beds. I'll be perfectly fine. Remember, my first Fleet tour was when you were in diapers, young man." The corners of her eyes crinkled as she smiled. "And I've got two junior electromancers who have been practicing blowing out systems since the convocation where you showed me what you were up to. So you get the Warlady-Elect to send a flyer for us, and we're in."

"Rani, I don't know how to thank you," Jauffre began.

"You do too. A nice bottle of aged plum wine will do nicely."

"I promise I'll send the best," Jauffre said.

"Good. Then I'll see you up there," Rani cut the connection before he could reply.

Jauffre took a deep breath. Three towers down. Eleven to go. He'd known he could count on her, but he hadn't let himself consider how much her wholehearted support meant to him. He'd been nearly thirty when he'd first met her and wondered at first if she were his female progenitor. Rani had disabused him of that but satisfied his curiosity in many ways. She was the younger half-sister of his female progenitor and knew her well. She'd carried verbal messages between them for twelve years, until his female progenitor's death during the war. He never met her, but through Rani he felt he knew her, and that she had known him and been proud of the man he was. That Rani hadn't hesitated meant the world to him.

If they won, the restrictions would be loosened even further—

Sandrine had promised him that, and above all she would keep her word. Sai would know his mother.

Jauffre had just finished the calls when the young acolyte, Elen, came in. "Master Castal-Edo?" she said. "The Hierophant said to tell you that there was a missile in the lower robing room for you."

"Ah, wonderful," Jauffre said, getting to his feet. He hadn't gotten quite enough for every ship, but nineteen electromancers had promised to come on short notice, which was better than he'd expected. "Let's go see, shall we?"

Elen was obviously eager to come along. She looked like she was about to pop with curiosity. "Why is there a missile in the robing room?"

"You'll see in a minute." Since Jauffre had no idea where the lower robing room was, it was certainly useful to go with Elen. She chatted the entire way through the back passages that served the holy public rooms of the Sema. At last they emerged into a large, windowless hall below ground level, a few racks of clothing hanging in dust covers at one end, some chairs stacked neatly. In the middle of the room on a transport cradle was a 500, its indicator lights blinking that it was active but not armed, the way that it would be for transport to a ship or in storage aboard.

"That is so pos," Elen said.

"It's a pretty thing, isn't it?" Jauffre walked around it, fully twice his height and about as wide. Yes, a standard newer model, like the ones they'd had on *Golden Promise*.

"Is it real?" Elen asked. She touched its smooth skin cautiously.

"Absolutely," Jauffre said. "It could destroy most of the building if it exploded. But it's not armed." Yes, standard guidance systems, not the old, clunky ones. He examined it without touching, reading its indicator board.

"My mother let you have a live missile that could blow up the Sema in the lower robing room?" Elen said incredulously.

"Well, the first thing I'm going to do is physically disconnect the arming circuit so it can't be armed accidentally," Jauffre said. Carefully, he opened the indicator plate, checking the tangle of wires and circuits. Yes, that one carried the command to arm the missile. He lifted the yellow wire with one finger, tracing its course with his mind up the side of the missile toward the nose. And there was where it connected. A tiny push, physically shorting out the wire and burning it through. "Perfect," Jauffre said. "Now if anyone wants to arm the missile, they're going to have to replace the wiring first." He smiled at Elen. "So it can't blow up."

"It can't?" Elen looked more curious than alarmed.

"No," Jauffre assured her. He thumped the missile's nose. "It carries solid explosive. It has to be detonated by an electrical pulse. Normally, it's set one of two ways: either to detonate at a certain range which is set before launch, or by the sensors in the nose, which tell it to detonate when it impacts a solid surface. This is why countermeasures work. They convince the sensor that it's hit its target rather than scrap. The third way to detonate it is by a pulse from the ship that launched it, telling it to detonate when the weapons officer wants it to, but that's rarely used in battle when there are multiple missiles running at the same time. I've just shorted the wiring that tells it to detonate. Without that, it's harmless."

Elen walked around the missile's nose, one hand trailing on its smooth surface. "So what do you need it for?"

"I have nineteen electromancers who have volunteered to help protect the ships in our fleet by destroying incoming missiles. Most of them have never practiced on a real missile. So I asked the Warlady for a real missile. When they get here, I'm going to show them how to feel for the guidance controls as well as the arming circuits. It's not always safe to simply blow it up. If, for example, the missile were close to your ship."

"I understand," Elen said. "Then you want to turn it or something."

"Precisely. But that's harder. Arming is on or off. Guidance is multiple systems in three dimensions. So they need to feel what it's like on a real missile."

"Feel?" Elen put her head to the side.

"It's hard to explain. I can feel the way currents run." Jauffre shook his head.

"That's mega-pos!" Elen said, sounding for a moment exactly like Boral. Well, she might be three years younger than Boral, if that.

Jauffre smiled. "You're a Dreamer, aren't you?"

"Yes," Elen said. "Like my mother."

"Then I can show you, if you like. You can feel my perception." He held out his left hand. "Want to see?"

"Absolutely!"

"I assume you've connected to another Dreamer as part of your training," he said.

"Yes, Master Castal-Edo." Now she sounded like one of his apprentices.

"Good. This works very much the same way. Put your left hand under mine." Elen stood beside him, stretching out her left arm beneath his, almost touching. "Like that." He could feel the minute electrical impulses of the nerves in her hand, feel her reaching for the connection, her hand in his like a child being shown how to trace letters. "There."

The connection was strong and swift. "I have it," Elen said. Her face was sharp with concentration.

She'd been trained well, Jauffre thought. He would expect no less of the Hierophant's daughter. "Perfect," he said. "Now see what I see." He closed his eyes, reaching for the missile's guidance systems. They were there, beneath the missile's skin and their joined hands, networks of fibers carrying information to and from the processor to the steering thrusters, to the main thruster behind. There were forty of them, but he could make them resolve into clear channels, like arteries and veins converging on a heart. A bright convergence. He shared it with Elen. "There. That's the cluster leaving the processor for the thrusters. Blow that out and the missile can't steer. You see?"

"Yes, Master." Elen's voice was quiet, her connection louder than her words.

"And there's the feedback cluster coming in from the nose sensors. That lets the processor know when the missile has hit something. The easiest way to detonate an armed missile is to tell it that it's hit its target. You reach for that, there." He punctuated it by giving the sensor a shove, a tiny spark of electrical energy to the feedback cluster. Systems shifted, the processor sending a detonation order through the circuits, fizzling when it hit the shorted line just before the detonator. Jauffre opened his eyes, smiling, and let go of her hand.

"That is so positive!" Elen was grinning. "And if you hadn't shorted out the line first, it would have blown up the Sema!"

"And killed us," Jauffre said. "So I do try to be careful with it. That's why I shorted the detonator before anybody starts practicing."

"That was a really good idea." Elen's smile didn't fade. "Thank you for showing me. That was interesting."

"You are very welcome," Jauffre said. "If you'd like to come by later, I have two apprentices about your age who will be practicing. It's useful to see how skills other than one's own work."

Elen's smile disappeared, a serious look replacing it. "Thank you. I will, Master."

"Of course," Jauffre said. "Now if you don't mind, do you think you could greet Master Rani Castal-Horst when her flyer gets in in a few minutes and escort her and her apprentices to guest quarters? I think she would appreciate the gesture."

"Consider it done," Elen said. She hurried off, and Jauffre buried himself in the missile's circuits. He needed to be completely familiar before he showed anyone else.

Chapter Ten

Sandrine and the Nautarch bent over a screen the size of a large table, plots on it showing the entirety of the Morriganian system with the exception of the outermost uninhabited satellites. Lugh, the system primary, was a golden sphere. The Belt, a chain of installations and stations just outsystem of the fifth planet, glowed yellow on the plot. Insystem, Orbitals One through Seven made a secondary cordon around Morrigan, Orbital Seven as far out as a small moon would orbit, if Morrigan had one, while Orbitals One through Four snugged up at an altitude of four hundred kilometers.

The Nautarch scratched his chin. "In the last war, they usually jumped in outsystem on the opposite side from our gas giants. There's too much gravitational noise for a clean jump anywhere near them. If I were guessing, I'd guess that's what they'll do this time too."

Sandrine nodded. "I remember. But Altissimus Iulus is supposed to be more aggressive than Altissima Gnea was. She didn't want a defeat more than she wanted a victory."

The Nautarch snorted. "You said that right."

"If I were Iulus," Sandrine said, "I'd jump in just outside the Belt, try to overwhelm one of the platforms in the first shots, and then charge through the gap."

"But if they don't succeed quickly, then they have a problem. If they get stuck between us and the Belt, they'll be boxed with fire on both sides and gravitational soup to try to jump out of." The

Nautarch frowned at the screen. "One of his big advantages is his numbers. We can expect to see twenty-five ships or more."

"That many after Eresh? You think he'll use everything he has?"

"Wouldn't you?" the Nautarch asked. "That's why they're amassing at Cassandreia. I'd throw the whole thing at us. He's got to know how many ships we have. Less than twenty, he's fighting at losing odds, so why do it at all? He's a decisive man. I think he'll gamble their entire fleet."

Sandrine nodded slowly. She had never met him, never spoken with him personally as the Nautarch had. It made sense. "So what we have to do is close as quickly as possible."

The Nautarch raised an eyebrow. "Against larger numbers?"

"Our advantage is the electromancers. They're only helpful at short range. If we have to stand off and take barrage after barrage, they'll take us out. We have to be as aggressive as he is."

"That's risky."

Sandrine gave him a sideways smile. "It certainly is."

"Close, grapple and board." The Nautarch shook his head. "Hand to hand."

"That also negates their missile advantage if they outnumber us," Sandrine said. "If we're in close, they risk hitting their own ships. And you know they're not going to use the heavy ordnance, the 750s or 900s, if they're practically grappled. They'd blow themselves up too. If they're going to use that advantage, they have to stand back and lob them at us."

"Agreed." The Nautarch looked over the plot again. "I need an astrographer's exhaustive list of jump points."

"There are going to be a lot that are marginal," Sandrine said, "given the position of the outer planets. Unfortunately both of the inner planets are on the other side of Lugh at the moment. Now, if they're willing to jump to a marginal point, they have a great many options."

"That would be foolish. If anyone's slightly off-position in the jump, they'll come out in a gravity well or too close to the primary or something equally lethal. And you know with a big formation there's always the problem of micro-gravitonic interference from other ships. I wouldn't risk a marginal jump with a large formation."

"Nor would I," Sandrine said. "But I have no ships to burn."

"And wouldn't," the Nautarch said sharply. "We don't sacrifice our people pointlessly."

"We don't have people to burn either," Sandrine said. "They're what? Eight billion people? And we're close to three hundred million?"

"Above eight billion if you count the Adelphi Rim," the Nautarch said. "They've pressed client states into service. They've got troops to waste."

"Which we don't," Sandrine said. "And we're only going to have twenty electromancers." She shook her head. "We don't have most electromancers trained for missile defense, and there's no way to get it done in a day. But Warlady Dariah at least let them convene enough that there are twenty who can do it."

He gave her a speculative look. "And Castal-Edo can't train them?"

"He can. But not this afternoon," Sandrine said. "There are nineteen coming in, some already arrived and some on their way, who will run through a refresher course before they go to the ships. Training electromancers takes time, just like any other specialist. You wouldn't trust your ship to a pilot with an afternoon's training, would you?"

The Nautarch shrugged. "Obviously not. Well, it's twenty more electromancers than the Calpurnians have."

"That's what I say," Sandrine said. "I've led boarding parties with an electromancer before. I'll do a full briefing on it for the captains, once we get up there and talk about how to coordinate. Best practice is to use them as a missile shield until you're grappled, then get them in the boarding party if feasible."

"If feasible?"

Sandrine sighed. "Several of them are over sixty. They're among the most skilled, but obviously not people you'd choose to take into a melee. So they must be missile shield only."

"The Calpurnians won't be expecting that," the Nautarch said.

"Because nobody's seen it since Khreesos's day," Sandrine said. "We have a few surprises up our sleeves yet."

It was after planetary midnight when Sandrine finished her last meeting. She had a little less than six hours until it was time to go aboard *Immortal Fire*. Sleep would be welcome. She made her way to her room quickly through the nearly deserted corridors. Hopefully nobody would find anything they needed from her for at least four hours. She palmed open her door, then stopped short. It was dark and there was the sound of someone breathing. Her heart raced, and she turned the light on quickly.

Jauffre turned over in her bed. "What?" he said muzzily. He seemed to be sleeping in his clothes, his high-heeled boots on the floor looking somewhat the worse for wear.

"Nothing, my dear," Sandrine said. She turned the light back off and closed and locked the door. Of course an electronically locked door was no barrier to Jauffre.

"I have no idea where my guest quarters might be," he said sleepily. "And it seemed a lot of trouble to find someone and ask."

"So I suppose we are forced to share a bed," Sandrine said. She sat down on the edge of it and took her own boots off. "Is that not what usually befalls the protagonists of a romantic adventure?"

"What?" Jauffre muttered.

"Never mind." She smiled as she took her socks and jacket off, then crawled under the covers next to him. "You're asleep."

"Um."

She snuggled up to him, back to back, warmth to warmth. How often had she wanted to end the day with him since the end of the war? Now she could, Sandrine thought, for at least a few hours. It was easy to fall asleep listening to him breathe.

Jauffre awoke, momentarily disoriented. The sounds were wrong, the darkness the wrong shape. And there was Sandrine sleeping against him, spooned in his arms, her hand holding his around her waist as though afraid he'd vanish. The ventilation system sounds were quiet, soft white noise in the background. It was certainly not the only time he'd woken beside her.

He'd set out to seduce her the first time, exerting all his charm and flattery to tempt her. She was his guard, he her ward. She knew better. But it was hardly the first time he'd seduced someone with power over him. It gave him some control of the situation, which he desperately wanted.

Sandrine had hardly been an onerous task to set for himself. She was beautiful, with strong features and dark eyes, whip-smart and daring. She loved romantic stories and dramatic gestures, tales of honor and adventure and love that made her shed tears. Courting her, seducing her, was fun. And then there had been that moment, after having gotten his hand under her clothes, of watching her lose herself and break against his clever fingers, when there was nothing but the pleasure in giving her this, in seeing her face change at the apex, in her perfect trust. Her eyes opened, wide and blazing, and he was pretending to pretend to passion, caught in his own web.

He'd confessed it later. It was after they'd retaken *Golden Promise* but before the end of the war. By then she had been acting captain but still shared the cabin they'd been assigned as guardian and ward. They had been playing with fire, walking on the edge of love and pain and humiliation. They'd bitten too close to the bone, and he had pulled away, lying on his stomach with his face against the pillow, trying to breathe through it.

"I'm sorry," Sandrine had said, not touching him at any point. "My dear, I'm so sorry. If I knew where the edge was…."

He had lifted his head, glad the semi-darkness masked his expression. "I don't know where it is," he had said too truthfully.

"I see you don't. I can't know if you don't. I can read your body and listen to your breath. But I can't know how far is too far."

"Then we go over the edge," Jauffre had said. His heart had been slowing, coming down from a frantic peak. "I don't know where it is until I hit it. But I won't give this up. I won't let anyone control me that way."

"I see that, my love." Her voice had been gentle.

He had taken a breath. "No shackles."

"Never," Sandrine had promised. Then she had hesitated. "My dear, you don't need to do this."

"I started it, didn't I?" Jauffre had heard the hard note in his own voice, guilt and shame entwined. "I set out to seduce you for better treatment. It's not the first time. I'm very good at making myself pleasant."

She had swallowed like she'd taken a body-blow sparring. "I see."

"It wasn't difficult. You're so lovely." He had dropped his face against the sheets.

"And now?" Sandrine's voice had been even, as though she'd returned to guard after a painful hit.

"Well, I'm caught in my own trap, aren't I? I meant to use you. But you're so sincere and honorable you can't even imagine that someone else might not be. You're the real thing. You really are honest and brave and kind and just, and how could I not fall in love with the hero I've always presumed to be imaginary?" Jauffre had lifted his head, turning onto his side.

Sandrine had been tight-lipped. "And yet look at me, sleeping with my ward when I know it's wrong. We are supposed to be better than this. No one should ever have hurt you."

Jauffre had shrugged. "Whenever people have absolute power over others, there are always some who abuse it. It's human nature." He had raised a hand to the side of her face. "And there are others who don't." She had turned her face against his hand, his Sandrine whom he had hurt with his confession. He had known her then. He had known how far she had let him within the tight security perimeter around her heart. "I know you would never purposely hurt me."

"I don't want to," she had said.

"But you like to play with fire. And so do I. Out on the edge of the abyss it's dangerous." He had sat up, naked and exposed. "That's what makes it…"

"…so intense. So necessary," she had said, her hand over his.

"Yes." The guilt had squirmed round again. "I am sorry I meant to deceive you."

"As long as it's not deception now." Her hand had tightened suddenly on his, her mouth hardening. "You could run," Sandrine had said. "You could take the ship's dispatch boat. I could give you the codes and not pursue."

"My love, I can't fly a dispatch boat."

"We could run together." Sandrine had lifted her chin. "I'll check out the dispatch boat and say that I'm going to confer on another ship. I'll take you aboard. That's completely legitimate. And then we'll jump outsystem. We could go somewhere far away. Menaechmi. Eresh. Nobody would know who we are or ever find us."

She had meant it. For a moment the illusion had swum before his eyes. What if they ran like the lovers in the stories, went off to be pirates together, spending their days in warm places, hardy buccaneers who pillaged their way joyfully through life? Only it wasn't really like that, was it? Pillage left blood and burned bodies behind. There was no freedom without the cost, other lives ended, others left in pain. Stealing was all very well, except for the person stolen from. And Sandrine—her pride was in her service. She was good, better than even she realized, bright and shining like a polished sword. Sandrine without her honor and her purpose would not be Sandrine.

And in that instant he had known the script. He had known the lines of the part he played, one more deception. "My love," Jauffre had said, brushing the hair back from her forehead. "We'd never get away with it. They'd come after me. I'm a weapon, remember? My genes are too valuable. The only way we could do it is to hide somewhere and for me to never use my abilities again, and that would be intolerable."

"They would, but…"

"We wouldn't get away. They would hound me for the rest of my life and take me down like a mad animal." He had made his voice even and had met her eyes squarely. Because they wouldn't have. They could have done it. They could have made it, maybe. Probably. And she would have regretted it eventually, regretted the ruin he had made of her life, of everything she had been and might be. "It's better this way," Jauffre had said.

Sandrine had nodded. He had expected her to say something sweet, like how she loved him. Instead, she had gotten that stubborn look again. "I will change it," she had said. "I swear to you before all the gods, I will change it. I will make it so no one can hurt electromancers with impunity again."

"Sandrine—"

"My oath on it. I will make it different. I'll break anyone under me who abuses an electromancer. I'll change the guardianship. I'll be Hierarch someday, and I'll change the Black Guard."

"I expect you will," Jauffre had said. The other paths were opening out, not sunlit horizons but a thousand other roads through the stars.

And one of them had led here. Jauffre tightened his arm around sleeping Sandrine. She was Warlady. She would fulfill her oaths if she lived to do it. And she would live and thrive if he had anything to say about it. He bent his face against her hair, taking in the scent of her, the warmth of her trust. He'd have her back, no matter what came. He closed his eyes and slept.

It was an entrance, Jauffre thought, worthy of a play. The Warlady Sandrine came aboard *Immortal Fire* in an ordinary uniform, the rams' horns on her breast the only ornament, her sheathed blade worn on her left. She looked small between two fleet troopers with boarding pikes, a pair of Black Guards behind her. And then there was the electromancer at her side, all in gray with a sash of silver. *Immortal Fire*'s captain, a tall young man with a neatly trimmed mustache, had assembled the officers and senior crew to greet her. To his surprise, Jauffre recognized him.

"Captain Danzi-Jean," Sandrine said as he went to one knee before her, fist on his forehead. "Rise, and introduce me to your officers." Her voice was perfectly level. Of course she'd known the captain's name before she came aboard, or possibly she'd chosen him herself: Danzi-Jean, her former aide who had walked in on them so embarrassingly five years ago.

"Your Graciousness, you do me much honor," he said, and began the litany of introductions. When he had done them all, and Sandrine had a word for each, his eyes fell on Jauffre. "Master Castal-Edo, welcome aboard *Immortal Fire*."

"Thank you, Captain," Jauffre said. Danzi-Jean's eyes were frank and did not evade. He both remembered him and did not seem surprised to see him at the Warlady's side, the light gaming piece on the board beside the dark.

"I would like to see your command center," Sandrine said.

"Of course, Your Graciousness." Danzi-Jean led the way as the Guard aides she'd brought peeled off to take her things to her quarters.

Immortal Fire was by far the largest ship Jauffre had been on, more than twice the size of *Golden Promise*, and built as a warship, not a converted merchanter. Danzi-Jean walked ahead of him with Sandrine, proudly explaining that there were four missile tubes for 900s mounted in pairs dorsal and ventral plus a rear-facing 500 and a pair of forward facing 250s as bow chasers. *Golden Promise* had only mounted four 500s. The command center was in the middle of the ship where only a critical hit would reach it, a large half-moon chamber with twelve acceleration couches and screens that wrapped one-eighty around the front. Everything was new and pristine. The couches were creamy light tan leather embossed with *Immortal Fire*'s emblem of leaping flame in a brazier, the same as was painted on her black exterior on either side just aft of the main airlocks.

Sandrine stood patiently while he introduced her to each of the command crew and showed her the couch reserved for her, just to the right of the captain's own. The ship had been built to accommodate a flag officer, clearly. "I will require an acceleration couch for the electromancer as well," Sandrine said.

Danzi-Jean only checked for a moment. "In the command center, Your Graciousness?"

"Yes," Sandrine said. She looked at him. "Castal-Edo, perhaps this is a good time to demonstrate why electromancers have been assigned to twenty of the twenty-two ships in our fleet?"

"Of course, Your Graciousness," Jauffre said, giving her a look which he hoped wasn't ripe with panic. He really would have preferred to try this without the entire ship's company watching.

"Captain, please ready a 250 in one of the forward tubes. Turn off automatic acquisition and set it to detonate at one hundred kilometers. That should be well short of any other ship." Jauffre blinked. One hundred kilometers was a very long distance. If they hadn't been completely surrounded by watching crew, he would have protested.

"Yes, Your Graciousness," Danzi-Jean said. "Weapons, please prepare a 250 to fire on the Warlady's order."

He'd have to get it long before one hundred kilometers. That was five times his best range. "Use the Red Glove," Sandrine said under her breath.

"Yes. Right." Carefully, Jauffre drew the embroidered gauntlet onto his left hand, feeling the tiny electrodes embedded in the material against sensitive finger pads, as though he wore an interface, or the ghost of one. Here, in close orbit, he could feel the wisps of it around him, and wondered for a moment if Sister Leonie felt this all the time.

Thinking summoned her. Leonie's face swam into his mental vision, looking up as though startled through the whorls of Windfollower's mesh. "Yes? Is something wrong?"

"Just testing," Jauffre said, letting go of the connection.

"Just testing what?" Danzi-Jean asked.

"I didn't realize I was speaking aloud," Jauffre said.

"I've never seen an electromancer with a Greater Gift," Danzi-Jean said. Meaning of course he'd never seen an electromancer allowed to touch one.

"This is the Red Glove," Sandrine said. "It's meant for an electromancer, just as some gifts are designed for Dreamers. It amplifies his natural gifts, just as the gifts for Dreamers amplify theirs. Now we will see what it does, Captain." She glanced at the weapons officer. "You may fire when ready."

Jauffre closed his eyes, shutting out the distraction of the entire command crew watching curiously, wondering if he would fail. And if he did, what was he going to say? He would have plenty of words for Sandrine later for putting him on the spot like this.

"Firing a single 250," the weapons officer said.

Jauffre saw the shape of the ignition, though *Immortal Fire* was too large to actually feel a forward missile tube fire. New electronic systems came online, guidance and propulsion. It was clear of the tube, running free in front, racing away…it would be gone if he didn't push….

"The missile has gone dead," the weapons officer said. "Propulsion out. It's purely ballistic. It has a full system shutdown."

Jauffre opened his eyes. Sandrine was speaking. "If that were an enemy missile that had acquired on us, or was simply incoming, it's dead. And Castal-Edo could have detonated it just as easily. Only not a good idea right under our nose." She gave the command crew a smile. "So that's why we need an electromancer in the command center. Nobody's seen countermeasures like this since Khreesos's day."

The latter was perhaps an exaggeration. This had been done for at least a few generations, but that was still six hundred years in the past. Jauffre drew off the Red Glove as everyone stared at him.

"You may detonate it now," Sandrine said to the weapons officer. "It's at eighty kilometers. It won't damage anyone."

"Yes, Your Graciousness." The missile blew up on the forward screen very satisfactorily.

"That seems…extremely useful," Danzi-Jean said. "And there are electromancers on nineteen other ships?"

Sandrine nodded. "Yes, though Castal-Edo is the one who perfected this technique and who wears the Red Glove. The others should be able to provide some protection to the crews they serve with."

And that was a lovely way of putting it, Jauffre thought. The crews, not the ships. There was always the suspicion that the Black Guard wasted lives in the Fleet, but of course Sandrine knew that. She'd been a captain in the last war. Every word she said would be repeated. She was saying the right ones. He made a mental note to tell her that she might think herself clumsy at politics, but not nearly as much so as she thought.

"There will be a full briefing for the captains in four hours or so," Sandrine said. "Several are coming aboard, including the Nautarch, and the rest will attend virtually. I will see you in my office at that time. We'll discuss the integration of the electromancer techniques in detail." She turned to leave the command center. "I'll need a dedicated communications channel between now and then with full encryption. I need to speak with other ships as well."

"I'll route that to your office, Your Graciousness," Danzi-Jean said.

"Thank you. And I will see all of you very soon." Sandrine left the command center, Jauffre spinning about to follow at her heels, closer than the two Fleet troopers who scurried after. Sandrine turned back to them in the corridor. "I don't require escort between here and my quarters. You are free to stand down."

"Warlady…"

"I have been aboard *Immortal Fire* before," she said. "I know where I'm going."

They left the two troopers, Jauffre hurrying to catch up with Sandrine as she strode down the corridor. "I don't appreciate not having a moment's warning," Jauffre said in a low voice at her shoulder.

"Can't perform under pressure?"

"I assure you, dear lady, that's never been my problem." They rounded a corner into one of two parallel spines heading aft.

Sandrine gave him a wicked glance. "Do you think the Calpurnians are going to stroll in and let you line everything up perfectly while you feel relaxed and comfortable? If you can't do it now, you can't do it then. Best to find out."

"You're brutal." They stopped at the door for it to scan her hand. "And I believe you're enjoying this."

"If I can't do it now, I can't do it then either," Sandrine said as the door opened. "And now I'm going to get on with each captain individually before the briefing. I suggest you check with your electromancers and see if anyone is having a problem. I'm sure some crews are more accommodating than others. You can use the screen in the bedroom."

"Right. We let electromancers use screens and call up fleet-wide communications." Jauffre shook his head.

"We do now," Sandrine said.

Chapter Eleven

private shower was a tremendous luxury on a starship. Sandrine leaned her head back, feeling the warm water run through her hair, squelching the guilt that this was the Warlady's shower. That this was Dariah's shower. Dariah was dead, and truthfully she hadn't been aboard *Immortal Fire* in months. There was nothing that was hers here. This was not the first time Sandrine had been assigned the quarters of an officer now dead. It was simply the first time it had been someone she had known and cared for.

Sandrine took a deep breath, closing her eyes as the water flowed down her face. This was the Warlady's shower, and she was the Warlady. It was her pleasure to get clean after four days of running about. There simply hadn't been time for anything of the sort at the Sema. It had been hard enough to find time to sleep a few hours and put on clean clothes, and that had been nineteen hours ago.

Ship's time was the same as planetary time. It was very late. They kept watch inside the Belt. Sometime in the next three or four days the Calpurnian fleet would arrive. And then they would fight for their lives. Until then, there was no point in remaining at battle stations.

It was not what Khreesos would do, exhausting people with unnecessary alarms rather than saving them for the real fight. The thought slid through her mind. Her own? That of the Presence? Or simply her understanding of what Khreesos would have thought based on his tactics? Sandrine shook her head under the water. It didn't matter, not really. What mattered were the results.

She stepped out of the shower and dried herself, carefully clipping the drying cloth so that it wouldn't fall if it wasn't stowed before a jump, changing into sleeping clothes. They had managed to get the luggage to her quarters without delay or loss, a perk of being Warlady. She'd hunted her bag all over the ship more than once in the past. She slid her hand over the light panel and stepped out into the main room.

Jauffre lounged in the big bed propped up on a bolster, a portable screen open in his lap, the covers around his waist. He wore a scarlet silk robe of some sort that left most of his chest bare, louche and smug.

Sandrine burst out laughing as she approached. "What in the world are you wearing? And where did you get that?"

"I brought it with me in my bag when I came to Holyrood." He patted the bed beside him invitingly. "I thought I might see you."

"We ended things five years ago."

Jauffre shrugged. "So we did."

She sat down, shaking her head. "I sent for you and said it was an emergency so you brought…." She gestured at the scarlet silk.

"You neglected to say what you wanted me for."

"So you assumed…."

"I hoped." Jauffre reached out and she slid in beside him, curling in tight with her head against his silk-clad shoulder. "I ask you, what kind of man has this made up for a woman he hasn't been with in five years?"

"A very foolish one," she said. It was right to hear his heartbeat, to slide her arm around his waist.

"Probably." He dropped his face against her hair. "I am never going to let you go again."

Sandrine drew a deep, shuddering breath. "No," she said, "you're not. If we win, I'll be a conquering hero. They love a conquering hero. I'll have the political capital to do what I want, and if I want you by my side, I'll have it. And if we lose, we'll both be dead and it won't matter. So no more sneaking around."

His voice was low and entirely devoid of humor. "My light, nothing would be a greater honor than to stand by your side."

She held him tightly, fierce and strong. "Yes. Always." Sandrine tilted her head up. She wanted to see his face. "I love you, Jauffre."

"That has been obvious for some time." His eyes were tender.

"You are insufferable and smug and arrogant and vain and the best thing that ever happened to me."

"You are a complete pain in the ass, and I adore you." And there was the kiss, bright as flame and twice as imperishable.

Sandrine leaned into him. "Stay with me," she whispered when their mouths parted. "Stay until the end."

"You're going to win," he said.

"No pressure."

He put his head to the side so he could look at her. "Four people you trust think so."

"How is that?"

"Me."

"You are no tactician."

"Sister Leonie, who seems shrewd," Jauffre said. "And then there's Blessed Khreesos himself who accepted you as Warlady. And if that isn't enough, have you considered that you were Dariah's choice, too? I'm sure she expected to live longer, but in the natural course of things wouldn't she have stepped down in five years or so? And there would be her hand-groomed chosen candidate, her Somatophylax, ready to take over? The only thing is that it's earlier than she expected. But she knew you were the right person to be the next Archegos. And of all people, she knew what the job required."

Sandrine rested her forehead against his cheek. "That does make me feel better."

"Get some rest, love."

"I don't know if I can." His warmth was comforting. And yet every frayed nerve screamed for action.

"You can't sit at battle stations for three or four days anymore than anyone else can," Jauffre said sensibly. "If you try to, you'll be exhausted before the battle starts." His fingers began a slow pressure on the back of her shoulder blade, finding the muscles taut with worry. "Rest. I'm mortally certain someone will call you at the slightest provocation."

Sandrine laughed. "So am I."

"Then close your eyes. Take a hundred deep breaths while I work on your back." His voice was quiet. She got to thirty-nine before she was asleep.

Sandrine was talking to the Nautarch on a secure line in her day cabin when Danzi-Jean cut in. "Warlady, Nautarch, we are picking up disturbances inside the Belt insystem of Belt 26."

"Insystem of the Belt?" Sandrine said. She wasn't certain she'd heard correctly.

"Gravity soup," the Nautarch said. "The bastard's trying it."

"Bring the fleet to battle stations," Sandrine said. Her heart was suddenly pounding. This was it. A cold clarity came over her, the elongation of time. "I'll be in the command center momentarily. Nautarch?"

"Battle stations!" the Nautarch said, and his line to her cut out as he turned to his command center.

Sandrine jumped from her chair, reaching the door as the claxon sounded, lights flashing. *Immortal Fire* went to full alert, Sandrine charging down the halls like every other member of the crew. She stopped outside the command center doors, pulling her tunic down and taking a deep breath. The Warlady should not seem ruffled. Then she strode in.

The three large screens showed exterior views, one with Morrigan rising half-eclipsed, the bright lights of one of the orbital stations around its dark side. Danzi-Jean already had *Immortal Fire* underway. "Get us inside the Belt now! We're on the wrong side," he said.

"Coming about, Captain," the helm said.

On the wrong side. They'd bet wrong. And yet as they watched, the first Calpurnian ships came out of jump, seven of them as the vanguard. Another eight followed, one following too closely, coming out of jump only a few hundred meters behind one of the first. Warnings must be sounding aboard both ships, jump-fuddled crews slow to respond. The follower rode up on the leader, colliding with a bone-shattering crunch. Sandrine winced, watching it as it overrode its fellow.

That was the problem with big formations. A jump was calculated to take a single ship from one point to another, accounting for the constantly changing gravity fields of large bodies. A clean jump point meant that there was no interference that would alter the arrival point by more than a few kilometers, nothing at all in the volume of space. However, a marginal jump point, one that already had significant interference like the ones inside the Belt, meant there could be more variation, and in a big formation a few kilometers could be deadly.

"Get us in there," Sandrine said. "And get me the fleetwide channel."

The frigate *Winged Explorer*, which had been at the back of the fleet, was now at the front. It had a clean shot past Belt 26. An aggressive captain, Sandrine thought, as it fired ahead of the general order, a 500 launching toward the Calpurnians. The missile struck a ship just coming out of jump, punching into the side just forward of the steering thrusters.

"Warlady, Captain, we have a third group coming out of jump," the astrogator reported. "Another group of eight for a total of twenty-three Calpurnian ships. All are frigates or larger."

"On our twenty-two," Sandrine said loudly. "Even odds." Though five of their twenty-two were scoutships or pinnaces, mounting much less weaponry and considerably smaller. Still, it could have been a lot worse.

"You have fleetwide in three, two, one."

"Morriganians, the enemy is before us," Sandrine said. "They will try to break through. We will not let them. We have stood against them before and sent them running like frightened children. We will do the same again." She nodded for the officer to cut the comm. "Get us in where we can do some good, Captain."

The Calpurnian formations were slower to respond. Were the crews disoriented from a long jump, or was it just that the formation was so big? Sandrine slid into her chair beside Danzi-Jean's, pulling up the plots on her small screen. If Iulus took the major risk of jumping inside the Belt, what was he thinking? A confident and aggressive commander, one known for taking risks....

Jauffre came in and took the couch that Danzi-Jean had moved in for him. He looked at her questioningly but didn't interrupt.

Iulus was going straight for Morrigan. That was the only answer. He was going to do what Altissima Gnea had never managed: bombard the planet itself. And now he was between the Morriganian fleet and home. There were the orbital stations, but they were no match for twenty-three ships.

Belt 26 was firing a 250 at the nearest Calpurnian ship, which did not return fire, only deployed countermeasures. That confirmed it. Their job wasn't to break the Belt, but simply run around it. As for jumping the Morriganian ships in closer, that was frankly impossible at the moment. The entire area between the Calpurnian fleet and the orbital stations was hopelessly distorted.

And there was the next move. She saw it like pieces on a board. Sandrine's voice was perfectly even. "Communications, get me *Python, Spider, Hornet, Scorpion,* and *Ray.* I want their captains on a split screen now."

"Yes, Your Graciousness." Danzi-Jean looked at her with surprise.

"The five smallest ships," Sandrine said.

"You have them, Warlady," the communications officer said, one of the screens splitting into pictures of the five cramped command centers. The largest, *Scorpion,* carried a crew of fifty-one, and the smallest a crew of twelve with a single 250 missile tube. Behind the young captain of *Spider,* she could see one of Jauffre's electromancers strapped into his couch, looking like little more than a boy.

"You are now Task Force One," Sandrine said. "*Scorpion,* you have the lead. You are to disengage with the Calpurnians if you have engaged and microjump to the other side of Morrigan, toward Lugh. There should be a zone where there is only marginal interference from Morrigan herself and Lugh, the inner planets being on the other side of the system at the moment. You are then to double back at all possible speed, putting yourself between the Calpurnian navy and Morrigan, and engage them in support of the orbital stations." She saw one of them blanch and continued. "Do not think that we are hanging you out to dry or sending you on a suicide mission. We will be attacking the Calpurnian Navy from the rear. But the orbital stations need reinforcement, and more importantly you must protect our cities and people. You all have electromancers. It's time to use them."

"Warlady." "Your Graciousness." The captains signed off, the screen blanking a second and then cutting to a camera view of one of the scoutships pulling out of formation, preparing to run up to the jump.

The Nautarch was on the other line, and Sandrine quickly explained. "And now we wade in," he said.

"We do. The general order is close and board."

Jauffre felt it like a vast moving web, all the ships and their signals, varying strengths and varying distances. There was *Immortal Fire* around him, a container of light. Its systems were a cradle moving through the dark. And beyond, another. And another. Forty-five ships moved, each with its own unique signature. There was Belt 26, Belt 25 and 27 close enough to feel as well. And there were missiles running, too many to easily touch, fired between ships further ahead. *Immortal Fire* had been toward the front of the formation facing outsystem, so now was near the back.

He saw one of the scoutships wink out, jumping too far insystem for his perceptions. *Spider*, he thought. In the moment that the captains had been on split screen, he'd seen Boral. He wished he hadn't suggested the youngest electromancers be assigned to the smallest ships, but he'd hoped they'd be the least engaged. He'd raised Boral from babyhood, except for the time he'd been away during the war. But it was pointless to worry about him now. He was nineteen, and this time he'd have to take care of himself.

Jauffre closed his eyes, sinking into the web of perception. The Red Glove extended it. Without it, he would have readily felt *Immortal Fire*'s lifeblood of electricity, known the presence of the ships that flanked them, been aware of a vast fleet action taking place, but he could not have isolated systems on neighboring ships, felt their computer cores and main engines as distinct entities. He felt *Immortal Fire* surge forward, its neighbors close at hand. They were moving to engage.

Jauffre opened his eyes again, perceptions flickering back to the command center. Sandrine was leaning forward in her chair, right foot ahead of her left as though she could walk the ship closer to its goal.

"Three in the back of the Calpurnian fleet are lagging behind," she said to someone on the comm. "Older ships of the line. Maybe confused crews, or just older and slower. *Blackbriar, Avatar, Phantom* and *Void Prophecy* will concentrate on those three. Close and board. *Immortal Fire* will support. Let's take them out."

Close and board was a call for an electromancer. Jauffre watched the ships growing larger on the main screen. *Blackbriar* was coming down on one from above, angling for the dorsal airlocks, while *Void Prophecy* was coming alongside.

There was still some considerable amount of distance between, enough for a targeted shot. Danzi-Jean thought so too. "Clear the forward missile tubes. A pair of 500s, please. Prepare to fire one on their main engines. Fire when ready."

The missile streaked away, acquiring on the lagging ship. Either it didn't have countermeasures or thought it was too close. It didn't even take evasive maneuvers. The missile slammed straight into the main engine, the explosion venting compartments to space. The ship's drive faltered, main engines and thrusters offline. A ragged cheer went around the bridge.

Blackbriar's captain's voice came over the comm. "Moving to board at the dorsal airlock."

Void Prophecy replied, "Coming up below you to the ventral airlock."

Sandrine nodded sharply. "Good work. *Avatar* and *Phantom*, on the others." *Phantom* was already homing on the next laggard, a 250 and a 500 running toward it.

Blackbriar clamped on, drones pulling it closer to the disabled ship. *Immortal Fire* began to pull past the three ships tight together. The third laggard was being chased down by another ship, one Jauffre didn't recognize.

Sandrine's eyes were already on the main body of the Calpurnian fleet ahead. "Can you identify the Calpurnian flagship?" she asked the first officer.

"Not yet, Your Graciousness."

Blackbriar had the dorsal airlock clamped and open, boarding corridor extended. *Void Prophecy* was being drawn in by its drones. A boarding action from two sides was the best possible scenario, Jauffre thought. Defenders would be squeezed and have to face two attack fronts. He'd been in an action in the last war with *Golden Promise* clamped to one side and a Calpurnian clamped to the other, one of the hottest fights he'd ever been in. He reached out almost involuntarily, knowing he was out of range to feel anything aboard it. Only he wasn't. The Red Glove extended perception. *A strange absence of signatures, a lack of power that wasn't about the main engines being out....*

"Something's wrong," Jauffre said aloud.

Sandrine glanced around at him quickly. "What?"

"There's not enough power aboard that ship."

"We took the main engine out," Danzi-Jean said.

"It's not just that. It..." He wasn't able to complete his sentence.

The Calpurnian ship exploded. The explosion began midship, then spread like a chain forward and aft. For a moment *Blackbriar* was silhouetted dark against it, and then the explosion ripped through the Morriganian ship and *Blackbriar* exploded as well. Shrapnel tore through *Void Prophecy*, still not quite clamped. It reeled, atmosphere and liquids venting to space, as though it bled into the void. It was pushed sideways, away from the explosion, debris falling free. Some of the debris looked like people in suits. Jauffre's breath caught. Of course—the boarding party had been clustered at the airlock nearest to the Calpurnian. Maybe some of the suits held in the rain of shrapnel. Maybe.

"Fireships!" Sandrine shouted, angry rather than cowed. "*Avatar, Phantom,* break off your attack! *Void Guardian,* break off!"

Jauffre felt ill. Rani Castal-Horst was the electromancer assigned to *Void Prophecy.* Surely at her age she wouldn't have been with the boarding party. Surely. And *Blackbriar*—that was Jian Eri-

Savarin from the tower at New Houston, like Jauffre a veteran of the last war. He'd been enthusiastic; Jauffre hadn't had to persuade him, just ask. Surely Rani hadn't been at the airlock.

Phantom was close to its target, *Avatar* further out, a missile running toward the Calpurnian's main engine. The missile hadn't hit yet when the target exploded. *Avatar* was too far to take much damage, but *Phantom*'s nose was shredded, atmosphere plumes clearly visible on the screen. Alarms would be sounding, compartments sealing against space, preserving some lives at the cost of others.

Reports were pouring in. Everyone was calling Sandrine. She had *Avatar*'s captain on screen. "If your damage is minimal, you will assist *Phantom* and *Void Prophecy*."

"Yes, Warlady."

Sandrine looked at another plot, shifting the screen. "*Void Guardian*, I told you to stand off! That ship is a fireship! Do not approach within seven hundred and fifty kilometers!" The third fireship was still running. "Take it out with missiles. It won't return fire. It has no crew."

The weapons officer looked over at her. "Your Graciousness, we have a firing solution on one of the capital ships."

"Fire when ready," Danzi-Jean said.

"Get us in there," Sandrine said. She glanced sideways at Jauffre. "Ready for missile defense?"

"Of course," he said.

Immortal Fire swept past *Void Guardian* which was firing from its dorsal tubes, a pair of 500s running for the third fireship.

"Your Graciousness, do you want us to fire on it?" the weapons officer asked.

Sandrine shook her head. "They've got it."

Both missiles hit amidships, and the fireship blew, bright and incandescent but not close enough to any other ship for harm.

"We have an incoming missile," warned the weapons officer.. "Looks like a 500."

Jauffre stood up. He could feel the shape of it, a 500 originally fired at another target that had acquired on them, nearly at the end of its fuel. Too far out still. Coming. Coming. At ten kilometers he reached. It was easier with the Red Glove than he expected, schematics coming clear faster, hundredths of a second as it approached. And there was the detonator, just as he had showed Elen. A quick puff, a short.

"Eight seconds to impact," someone said.

"It's deactivated," Jauffre said. For good measure he touched the guidance, the missile nearly upon them, adjusting minutely to slide beneath Immortal Fire harmlessly.

"The missile has missed us and is unguided," someone reported.

"Nice," Danzi-Jean said, sparing Jauffre a glance as they waded into the battle.

Sandrine rubbed her palms against her thighs, then put her right hand back on the little board on her chair arm. Four ships. She'd already lost four ships and the Calpurnians had lost nothing except hulks they intended to destroy. *Blackbriar* was lost with all hands. *Phantom* and *Void Prophecy* were probably complete losses, though some of the four hundred from each crew might be saved. *Avatar* was damaged and required search and rescue. And she had nothing to show for it. She must get this back on track. She had to think like a nautarch, not a captain. Their attack had been blunted by the fireships. Instead of a concentrated wedge driving into the Calpurnian rear, they were now an unruly sort of cloud behind the Calpurnian advance. *Blessed Khreesos*, she thought, *what would you do?* Of course there was no answer.

She opened a channel to the Nautarch. Originally in the rearguard, he was now in front with his ship, *Rising Light*. "Can you punch into the flank?"

The Nautarch shook his head. "I'd be six on ten, and if we get sandwiched between them, we're in real trouble. We need to swing further sunward, toward Morrigan, and try to get on their flank as they go in."

He knew his business, Sandrine thought, and he'd never been shy of engaging. If he said he couldn't punch through, he was probably right. "Do it then," she said. "I'll be on them with my five." Five, she thought. He had six, she had five, and there were five lighter ships coming around from the other side. Suddenly twenty-two on twenty-three was eleven on twenty. Iulus had greatly improved his chances. Or she had blown hers.

She glanced over at Jauffre, his expression taut as though he were listening to something she couldn't hear. No, she still had the electromancers, which meant her strategy had to be the same. "Danzi-Jean, bring us as close as possible to the nearest Calpurnian ship. We will close and board. Please ask weapons to fire as they bear."

"Yes, Warlady."

A tremendous amount of ordnance was flying as the ships ahead of her engaged. It was almost impossible to sort out whose missiles were whose. One of the problems was inaccurate acquisition. The Calpurnians were growing cautious about launching, given the tightness of the formation. They might hit their own. Meanwhile, on the longer-range plot, the front end of the Calpurnian formation was firing on Orbital Three. They were in range.

Around the curve of the planet came three small ships, *Scorpion* and *Spider* and *Ray*. They dodged in, *Ray* so small that it was essentially flying on maneuvering jets. A Calpurnian capital ship fired a pair of 500s on Orbital Three, enough to completely depressurize the station, laying berths and restaurants and quarters and technical core open to space. *Scorpion* darted in, and for a moment with bated breath Sandrine thought that the captain intended to collide with the incoming missiles, taking them out at the expense of her ship. And then one of the missiles died. Its engine cut out, swinging crazily sideways in Morrigan's gravity well. The second one swept past *Scorpion*, toward Orbital Three, and then detonated well short of its target.

Jauffre made a choked sound that was almost a sob. "Arlaine is seventeen years old," he said. "Seventeen."

"That is what electromancers can do," Sandrine said over the comm. "Get in close and let your electromancer work!" She looked at Danzi-Jean. His eyes said clearly, *because that's all we've got*.

The other two small ships were coming in now, sweeping around the curve of the planet. A Calpurnian capital ship fired, a 500 running true toward *Spider*. *Spider* went to full thrusters, the missile in pursuit. It looked as though it would run straight into it, but the heat of the full burn detonated the missile short. No doubt there was some minor damage, but the engine pod was the most heavily armored part of any ship.

Python took a crippling hit, a 250 shearing off missile launcher and dorsal thrusters, atmosphere pouring out. "We are in distress!" *Python*'s captain shouted. "We have limited helm control!" As Sandrine watched, *Python* dived into the atmosphere, a burning streak across the night side surely clearly visible from the ground. "All crew, abandon ship!" One, two...three lifecraft launched. *Python* fell like a burning meteor toward the Eastern Sea.

The other small ships were now weaving madly across the front of the Calpurnian advance. They were doing damage, Sandrine thought. She saw *Hornet* put a 250 through the main engines of one of the Calpurnian ships. It certainly wasn't enough to destroy it, but from the flame-out and sidle from thrusters on only one side operative, it was clear that the Calpurnian was adrift.

Spider had acquired a loose 250 fired earlier. It closed on the scoutship, unshakable, though *Spider* dodged. Jauffre's face was white. "Come on, Boral," he said quietly. "Concentrate." Too late. It was too close. The missile struck just forward of the engine pod, but instead of detonating it punched into a single compartment, failing to explode, its tail sticking out like a dart. Jauffre swallowed hard, and Sandrine saw him gripping the arms of his couch. "We've got to work on guidance systems," he said.

Sandrine took a deep breath. The small ships were doing their job. They were blunting the Calpurnian offensive. No doubt Iulus had expected to have the orbital stations out of the way by now, but instead he was having to waste ordnance and time on these gadflies. Just ahead of *Immortal Fire* was one of the largest Calpurnian ships, its ventral missile launchers taken out by fire. It could hardly fire the dorsal ones without the missiles acquiring on the Calpurnian ship above it before they could acquire on *Immortal Fire*. "Captain Danzi-Jean," she said.

She didn't have to finish. "Helm, take us beneath that ship," he said, then opened the comm. "Primary boarding party to the dorsal airlock."

"Do you want me in the boarding party or on missile defense?" Jauffre asked.

She paused. Jauffre in a boarding party was deadly, but with all the missiles running right this moment, his skills were needed there. "Stay on missile defense right now," she said.

CHAPTER TWELVE

It was as well she put him on missile defense, Jauffre thought. In the next three minutes he fended off two missiles as *Immortal Fire* maneuvered for a docking clamp. Once they were in position, they were locked to the Calpurnian. He heard the officer in charge of the boarding party calling Danzi-Jean on the comm. "We are having trouble with their airlock. If we use charges, we need to back off and retract the umbilical."

"I can get it from here," Jauffre said.

Sandrine raised an eyebrow. She knew he could do it with his hand on the airlock—but from a hundred meters away?

"Red Glove," Jauffre said. He closed his eyes. Finding *Immortal Fire*'s boarding umbilicals was easy. They were part of the ship's systems. It was simply a matter of tracing them. And there—there was the Calpurnian airlock, disabled manually so that it would not cycle. And there was the switch, the manual override that disengaged it, telling it that all seals were red and the other side of the airlock was simply vacuum, that there was nothing attached to the docking port. But of course there was. All he had to do was turn its sensors back on. *There.* There was a click and the airlock began cycling. "Got it," Jauffre said.

Down below, the boarding party would be rushing in, their vacuum suits snug against possible depressurization, the Calpurnian crew desperately trying to hold them at bay, energy flails bright in the strobing emergency lights....

"We have a 900 incoming!" the weapons officer said, his voice scaling up.

"Firing on us when we're attached to one of theirs?" Danzi-Jean said incredulously.

"Iulus doesn't care if he breaks eggs to make eggbread," Sandrine said evenly. "Castal-Edo?"

"Warlady," Jauffre said, reaching for the missile. It detonated exactly ten kilometers short, a shockwave rocking the ship but doing no damage.

"Return fire with the forward tube," Danzi-Jean said. "Clear and fire when ready."

"We have another acquisition," the weapons officer said. "500 running for our nose."

"Got it," Jauffre said. He closed his eyes, feeling for the guidance system this time. And there. There were the junctions, there the leads to the processor. A push, turning it away, toward the largest Calpurnian ship. He felt it acquire, felt *Immortal Fire*'s missile launch at the same time, the pair running toward the massive ship of the line in tandem, only a hundred and twenty meters apart.

He opened his eyes. The missiles struck home together, cutting through armor, deep into the ship's flank. A very rewarding explosion followed. A plume of fire showed, burning atmospherics fed from within, not yet snuffed out by the void.

"That's the flagship, Your Graciousness," the weapons officer said. "Warlady, we have a positive identification."

"Let the fleet know," Sandrine said. "We're already clamped and boarding another ship."

The flagship was bearing down on them, coming closer. To Jauffre, the missiles were like a cloud, a haze, fifty missiles live at once all over the place, thirty ships engaged in the immediate vicinity. So much electronics, so much energy…it was enormous and yet not overwhelming. He could still sort individual signatures, though the volume of it raised the hair on his arms.

The flagship fired again, another 900, another pair of 500s. It was giving *Immortal Fire* everything it had. They must have been identified, too.

Three missiles running at once, Jauffre thought. *I could get any one. Maybe any two.* He closed his eyes, trying to block out additional distractions. So much energy. So much wild electricity, so many missiles and so many ships. The Red Glove tingled on his hand, but this was his own perception, his wild need. His embattled children. Rani. Sandrine. A lifetime of fears and the inability to protect those he loved. It rose like tears. There was that well, deep in the core of him. *Yes, I am dangerous. If I let it go, unchain all the things so carefully held in check….* He could see the three oncoming missiles, feel *Immortal Fire* around him attached to the Calpurnian ship, feel the boarding party with their energy flails and pikes. It was all his, every charged ion, just like in that long-ago action in *Golden Promise*'s command center. Three missiles.

Jauffre opened his hands. It fed in through the right hand, energy drawn from the ambient around him, passing through his body into the Red Glove, into his left hand. He reached out and threw the lightning.

There was a hiss and pop as one of the viewscreens blew out from the current passing through it, through *Immortal Fire*'s skin, and then it raced across the void, indigo tendrils of current catching the 900 as it approached, arcing to the pair of 500s, all three missiles fried in a single burst. Every system in them seized, harmless pieces of metal on purely ballistic courses. Jauffre opened his eyes.

"Holy Khreesos," the communications officer said under his breath. Danzi-Jean was looking at him with an expression part horror and part amazement. Jauffre's legs were shaking with the amount of energy that had passed through him. He sat down heavily on the end of his couch.

Sandrine's mouth curved in a smile. She pitched her voice for the whole command crew to hear. "That, my friends, is what Holy Khreesos could do indeed. Now fire on the flagship! Give them every tube that bears."

The Calpurnian they were clamped to obscured the dorsal and forward tubes, but the ventral and aft tubes were clear. "Firing now," the weapons officer said. "Two 900s and a 500."

Immortal Fire was large enough that there was no kick, nothing one could feel from even so big a launch. But now the Calpurnian flagship was turning away. In a battle sometimes missiles acquired wrong. Sometimes they flamed out. Sometimes they failed to detonate. All of these things happening frequently was odd, but not impossible especially in the heat of combat. But lightning flashing across the void was inexplicable. Now Iulus knew something was wrong. *Immortal Fire*'s missiles ran true straight toward the flagship.

"Can you hit the flagship with lightning?" Sandrine asked quietly.

Jauffre shook his head. It had stopped ringing. He stood up. "Too far," he said.

She nodded. "Save it for missiles then." She smiled. "You slagged my viewscreen."

He gave her a little bow, fist on forehead, his eyes on hers. "I apologize profoundly, dear lady."

Three missiles slammed into the side of the Calpurnian flagship. It was heavily armored. It didn't explode, but split in half, the two sections limned in fire along the broken edge, fire abruptly quenched by vacuum.

The Nautarch's ship, *Rising Light*, closed on a capital ship, which fired a 900 at point-blank range. The 900 failed to detonate, clanging along the ship's side and tumbling away. In a moment, *Rising Light* had them clamped side to side, umbilicals pulling their airlocks together.

Another missile was running at *Immortal Fire*. Almost

carelessly, Jauffre detonated it at twelve kilometers. He closed his eyes, slipping into pure perception.

Sandrine leaned forward, her eyes on the two remaining screens. Data poured in, distances and bearings displaying transparently in a corner of each view. *Traveler* was damaged, its captain pulling back out of the main combat. *Phantom* had been destroyed. They had ten large ships in the battle plus four small ones. The Calpurnians were taking the worst of it in their turn, six disabled or boarded, with two destroyed. It was now ten on twelve, not counting the scoutships. The tide was turning Sandrine's way.

"Keep pushing," she ordered. "Keep the pressure on. Get in close." And they were doing it. The battle had moved closer to Morrigan, the orbital stations able to fire. She saw the change as it happened, a slow, rolling movement. The Calpurnian ships that weren't engaged in boarding actions changed course. Instead of trying to engage the Morriganian fleet, they were trying to stand back. Somebody had figured out the electromancers' range. It was better to move nearer to Morrigan and the orbital stations than to let ships with electromancers close.

"Captain, we have the command center," the leader of *Immortal Fire*'s boarding party said. "The ship is ours."

Danzi-Jean nodded sharply. "Excellent. Remain as prize captain and take it into Orbital Four as you are able. Seal the airlock on your end. We will release boarding clamps."

"Good," Sandrine said. "We need to stick with them. Don't let them get out of range and pound us from a distance."

Jauffre opened his eyes. "They've got to start running out of ordnance at some point. They can't carry infinite missiles."

"And you can stop infinite ones?" Danzi-Jean asked.

"No," Jauffre admitted. "Even I can't. And the others—there

are going to be some that get through."

"Some is better than most," Sandrine said. "Electromancers are the most effective countermeasures we have. And you're correct—even the largest ships have a limited number of missiles. At some point they will run short."

"And so will we," Danzi-Jean said.

"True," Sandrine said. "At which point we're at a draw and they'll pull out because we can close and board with the electromancers."

The captain nodded his agreement. "We have three prizes already," he said. "Though that does tie up the ships taking prizes."

"Warlady, we have an incoming call from the Hierophant," the communications officer said.

"Put her on the split screen," Sandrine replied.

Leonie's face appeared in the corner of the display, Windfollower across her brow. "We are showing Calpurnian ships within the perimeter of the orbital stations," she said. "My Lady Archegos, should we put out a full civil defense alert?"

Sandrine mentally cursed herself for not thinking of it. But of course she'd never done planetary defense. In the last war, she'd been assigned on shipboard the entire time. Leonie was prompting her, and she appreciated it. "Yes, as a precautionary measure," Sandrine said. "Since they are within the perimeter."

Leonie inclined her head. "Thank you, Your Graciousness." She cut the comm at her end.

Jauffre frowned. "Are they that close in?" he asked quietly.

Sandrine glanced at the plot. "Not yet," she said. "But they may be soon." She looked at Danzi-Jean. "Are we able to cast off from the prize yet?"

"In a few seconds, Your Graciousness."

"Then take us home, Captain," she said. "We will support the orbital stations. All ships that are able, pursue. Stay on them!"

Leonie heard the sirens go off, the high, shrill screams of civil defense claxons she hadn't heard since the last war. There had been drills, of course. Those had always been preceded by announcements, the sirens in tandem with a calm voice repeating that it was just a drill, would everyone go to shelters as they were able in order to best simulate conditions of an actual attack. In reality, few people had done so recently. It seemed unlikely that anyone would indeed be able to attack them. Even in the last war, when the alerts had been real, no missiles had actually fallen on Morrigan. Between the Fleet and the orbital stations, not a single missile had penetrated. *Perhaps,* Leonie thought, *we have grown too confident. Or perhaps the Calpurnians have grown more aggressive.*

That Sandrine was not doing as well as Dariah had done didn't bear thinking of. This Altissimus Iulus was much better than the previous commander. Even Leonie could see how aggressive this assault had been by simply watching the plots. Of all the people on Morrigan, perhaps she might be the one who best understood how grave their threat was this time. Thus, when the sirens sounded, she got up from her desk and began to walk calmly toward the nearest weather shelter in the sub-basement. Windfollower would allow her to monitor systems while she did so.

In the courtyard the lights were dimmed for planetary night, the images of the gods in their niches. The fountain played, its falling droplets reflecting the bright pixels of the images. People were actually hurrying, some calling and shouting to others.

Leonie looked up. There were clearly lights in the sky that shouldn't be there. Everyone was used to the orbital stations parading in their majestic courses around the world, but there were other lights moving against the pattern. Some were fast, their direction constantly changing. Leonie frowned, asking

Windfollower for information from air control, but it was unable to give any. They were not registered craft. They were enemy.

People were running now, a streak of fire across the sky like a meteor, green-tinged in the atmosphere as it sunk behind the mountain. Windfollower supplied information: a lifecraft, Morriganian transponder. Leonie's breath caught in her throat. Which ship had been destroyed? Who had lost their child today? Windfollower had no further information.

The sirens' pitch rose. Someone screamed, their voice echoing across the courtyard. Another streak of flame, this one getting larger rather than crossing the sky.

"Windfollower?" Leonie said aloud.

A missile has been fired on these coordinates, Windfollower supplied. *It is targeting the city of Holyrood. Impact in twenty-two seconds.*

Twenty-two seconds. Not enough to reach the shelter. Not enough to go far. Leonie looked around for what might be the safest place. Beneath the porticos? Or was that worse? The shelter of the columns or would they collapse?

And then her heart stopped. In a scramble of gray, someone was running against the flow, breaking free of the crowd to run up the stairs, toward the balcony with the clearest view of the sky and the waiting city beyond: Elen.

Leonie screamed. She had never in her life screamed aloud like this, not in the grip of childbirth. Elen bounded up the last steps, looking straight toward the city, toward the missile plunging like a ball of fire. She tilted her head up, then raised her left hand to the sky.

"Elen!" Leonie shrieked.

Probably she didn't hear her. Not over the mechanical warning. *Impact in eight seconds.*

"Elen!"

Elen's arm shook, her eyes closing. The missile exploded in the air six kilometers up, a fireball raining tiny pieces from high above rather than plunging into the heart of the city, and Elen crumpled to the pavement.

Leonie took the steps two at a time. Her head. Did she hit her head on the stone? She dove to her knees. Elen was shaking, her limbs trembling as though she'd touched a live wire. "I got it," she stuttered between clenched teeth. "I got it."

"Yes, my love. You did," Leonie said, getting her head into her lap. "Baby, you did." She didn't move until the medics came.

"Your Graciousness, missiles have been fired at planetary targets," the weapons officer said. "We have a missile aimed at Holyrood."

"Get us in closer!" Sandrine said, leaning forward. She glanced at Jauffre and he shook his head. It was far too long a range unless perhaps one of the electromancers on the speedy scoutships that were already practically on top of it….

"We have an atmospheric detonation," the weapons officer said.

Sandrine sighed with relief. "Fire on the attacking ships at extreme range," she said.

Danzi-Jean looked alarmed. "There is a high chance of the missile acquiring on one of our ships," he said.

"But our ships have electromancers who can turn them," Sandrine said. "Do it."

The forward tube fired, a missile streaking away into the void. Sandrine almost felt rather than saw the change, a shift in the pattern of engagement. It was different in some indefinable way, a break in the rhythm. A new order had gone out: disengage. One ship, then several, were attempting to break off. A dispatch boat pulled away from the shattered Calpurnian flagship, weaving its way swiftly through floating debris. One of the capital ships moved ponderously at half-power, beating its way outsystem toward one of the gaps in the Belt.

"Your Graciousness," the Nautarch said on the comm, "they're retreating."

"Stay on them," Sandrine said. "All ships that are capable, stay on them. Make them spend as much as you can. Keep throwing ordnance at them. Board if possible. Don't let them go."

"You heard the Warlady," the Nautarch said with approval in his voice.

Danzi-Jean was talking to the weapons officer. "Fire the forward tube as we bear."

"Captain, we are out of 250s."

"Then load the dorsal tubes," Danzi-Jean said. "How many 900s in reserve?"

"We have three more."

Sandrine shook her head. Three, and then they had only a few 500s for the aft tubes. "We'll run out of missiles before we run out of targets," Sandrine said, conscious of the positive effect of her words. "Their good fortune."

One of the smaller Calpurnian ships was almost on top of them as they began a run up to a jump. Jauffre stood up, reaching up with Red Glove, closing his fist. The Calpurnian's main engine died, an override circuit tripped. "Something to mop up," Jauffre said. He had a little smile on his face, a twist of anger showing as well as delight in his art. The communications officer was already calling for their surrender.

The Calpurnians were maneuvering now. The slow capital ship exchanged fire with Belt 21, trying to edge past it into open space. A dispatch boat jumped, small enough to need less room to avoid the gravity soup. The ships that were in close to Morrigan were madly trying to put distance between themselves and the planet's gravity well, though for most of them that meant going straight back into the Morriganian Fleet. Some broke in the other direction, toward Lugh. They'd make it, Sandrine thought. There was nothing to stop them, and if they went sunward they'd have plenty of space to jump before the primary's gravity field was too strong.

"Get me some numbers," she said. "What do we have?"

"Warlady, we have five ships destroyed or abandoned," Danzi-Jean's first officer said. "We have two more seriously damaged. There are ten more with damage reported though they are still engaged, and five without significant damage."

She'd trashed half the Fleet, Sandrine thought. She raised her chin. The reward had better be great enough. "And the Calpurnians?" she asked evenly.

"Seven destroyed or abandoned," she said, "Six taken as prizes or surrendered. One more too severely damaged to jump and adrift. All the rest have taken significant damage though they are underway."

"They've lost half their Navy," Danzi-Jean said. Even as he spoke, a frigate went to jump the moment it was clear of Morrigan. "Half the Calpurnian Navy."

"Half the Navy that was here," Sandrine said. "About a third of their total strength." It seemed impossible. A third of their total strength, a third of the strength of the mightiest empire. Another capital ship jumped, the missile following it continuing on its course. Three ships continued to race sunward, now out of range, running up on a jump point.

"And they'll be scattered all over," Sandrine said. "They're having to jump to wherever they can. There is no task force. They're simply escaping to any point they can get a clear window for." There was satisfaction in her voice. "It's a rout."

"It's the greatest victory in three generations," the Nautarch said on the comm.

"And thanks to the expertise and professionalism and courage of our Fleet," Sandrine said, "And your leadership, Nautarch."

"Thanks be to Blessed Khreesos," the Nautarch said gruffly, "Who has given us Sandrine Dal-Vesta."

The cheer that ran around the command center was nothing Sandrine had ever imagined. She looked around it, trying to be grave as she imagined Khreesos would have been. The pride and exhaustion on Jauffre's face made her smile. "I am the one who has received His blessing," Sandrine said.

Chapter Thirteen

Planetary morning was coming. The lights had come up in the courtyards and halls of the Sema. Jauffre entered the lower robing room. The missile had been pushed back against the wall, a plastic cover half over it. A table had been laid with the daymeal, plastic chairs unstacked, and the scent of tea rose above the oil and steel smell of the missile. Eight electromancers were here. He was the ninth. He stopped a moment in the doorway before they saw him.

Briony had one arm around Gaffar, a plastic bowl of tea in her other hand, while he leaned against her shoulder. He was Rani's son, five years Jauffre's junior, his blood kinsman. The expression on his face told all.

Arlaine saw him first, leaping up from a plastic chair and running to him. "Master!" she said, throwing herself into his arms. Boral followed, enveloping him in an embrace, oddly enough taller than Jauffre by a few centimeters.

"Children," he said, trying to keep tears out of his voice. "My dear children."

"Boral nearly got blown up," Arlaine said.

"But I didn't," Boral said.

"Arlaine, don't tattle," Jauffre said, squeezing them both tight. "And you did very, very well. Both of you. Arlaine, I saw you get one right after another with the orbital station. I couldn't have done better myself."

Arlaine pulled back. "Thank you. Thank you so much."

"And Boral, I saw you save the ship." He gave Boral's arm a squeeze.

"It was close," Boral said. "They're all glad."

"Not to be dead," Arlaine said.

"They all want to buy me a drink, was what the captain said," Boral said. "They said I was mega-positive and that electromancers were all pos with them. The captain wants to know if I can stay." He put his head to the side. "Can I? I'd really like to. *Spider*'s a good ship and I know it'll need repairs…"

"…because there's a big hole in the side…" put in Arlaine.

"…but I'd like to stay. Electromancers have been assigned to the Fleet before, and there's still a war!"

"But without a Black Guard to watch you," Jauffre said, feeling something loosen in his chest. "I don't see why an electromancer couldn't be part of a ship's crew as a specialist, just like the medic and the engineer. If you really want to, I can speak to the Warlady about it."

"I really want to," Boral said. "They're a super crew. And I'd like to, you know, get out of the tower and see the universe."

"So would I, Boral. So would I." Jauffre patted him on the back again. "I'll speak to the Warlady. But I think I will be staying here at the Sema. And you, Arlaine…."

"I know," Arlaine said with a resigned air. "Back to the tower."

Jauffre lifted her chin with one hand. "If I am staying here, my apprentices need to be here. So you are only going back long enough to pack and help the younger apprentices move. I think you will find Holyrood an interesting place to finish growing up."

"Oh." Arlaine hugged him tight. "You'll take us with you, Master?"

"I would never leave you," Jauffre said. He'd talk to Sandrine. She would allow it, and now nobody could gainsay her. In a moment he'd go speak with Gaffar. Rani had been dear to him, as his female progenitor's half-sister and their go-between, but she also had been Gaffar's progenitor and mother. Her loss cut deep.

"We'll never leave you either, Master," Boral said. He stopped, then went on. "No matter how far away we go."

"I know," Jauffre said. There would be grief, but there was also this. Rani would be proud to have died for their freedom.

Sandrine landed in planetary full day, though of course it was dark except for the bright lights of the landing zone. Her shuttle came into Holyrood's main port, too large for the courtyards of the Sema. *Immortal Fire* waited in orbit, Danzi-Jean beginning the repairs—not that there were nearly as many as there could have been.

She had seen the honor guard for the Warlady many times. She had arranged it as Somatophylax, had stood at the foot of the ramp while Dariah arrived on many occasions. This time it was she who walked down to the sound of all the pike butts striking the ground together, the Guard salute. It was she who was met fist on forehead. It was, Sandrine thought, deeply surreal.

All the nets were watching, broadcasting live. She walked through the corridor of honor guards in her dark uniform still sweaty from the battle, her chin held high. She was not watching to see who was out of place and if the vehicle was lined up. Those were her old duties as Somatophylax. She would need one of her own soon.

You will need loyal friends, someone whispered in her head. *There is nothing you need more.*

Blessed Khreesos? Sandrine thought, *Is that you?* Of course. She was now back in range of the Sema, in the range of the Presence. He had told her he could not reach her when she was on a distant ship.

Who else? He sounded amused. *Welcome home, Warlady. And what will you do now?*

Eat a meal, Sandrine thought. *See Jauffre. And then start changing the world.*

She could almost hear him smile as she stepped into the waiting vehicle. *And then?*

Sandrine leaned back against the cushions as an aide closed the door. *The Calpurnians are not done,* she thought. *Dariah wanted me to think of the endgame while still in the beginning, to understand the causes of wars rather than simply fight them. We've defeated a fleet today. But we have not changed the causes of the war. The Altissimi vie to deliver what cannot be done—constant growth based on constant expansion rather than equilibrium. Unless we can permanently change the way Calpurnia relates to its neighbors and the way its internal economic systems work, we have only put off the war. We will fight again and again if we do not solve the underlying problem. Agathos Daimon, I do not yet see how to do that.*

Nor do I, he admitted. *I am wise, not omniscient.*

I know, Sandrine said. *But the first step must be to peel off their allies. Unwilling client states and those they have conquered must be carefully detached. Menaechmi and Lono have no love of Calpurnia. If we can do that at least we will have made this victory more lasting. It will buy time for me, or for those who come after me, to find a better solution. And perhaps....* Sandrine stopped.

Perhaps you dream of doing as I did, Khreesos said. *Perhaps you have tasted victory and found it sweet.*

Sandrine bent her head. *Perhaps so,* she thought. *But first we rebuild. First we change ourselves. Then we change the universe as you did.*

Maps can be rearranged. Empires rise and fall. Even the gods do not know the end.

Only the beginning, thought Sandrine, and she looked out through the window of the vehicle at the crowds of Holyrood assembled to see their new Warlady.

Jauffre followed the green corridor to the doors to the Life Center, quite aware of the curious stares that greeted him. He supposed he cut quite a figure in his battle-worn silver-gray court dress, long leather coat and sash with silver thread. He had not had time to change yet.

The first person he saw when he opened the doors was the Hierophant, just coming out of the corridor to the private cubicles. She looked tired, as she must be with all that had happened, but not distraught, which was a relief in itself. "Jauffre," she said.

"Sister Leonie." He made a small bow for the benefit of the young healer on duty at the desk. "I thought that I would stop in and see how Elen is. I heard that she destroyed a missile and that she was in the Life Center. Please know that I had no idea when I showed her what I was doing with the guidance system that she had any abilities in that direction. I apologize for…"

"For giving her the skill to save us all?" Leonie asked. "Many people in Holyrood would be dead otherwise. And Elen will recover."

"How is she?" Jauffre asked.

"They are describing it as a case of overload. She is surprisingly well, considering. They want to keep her for observation and electrolyte therapy for a few more hours. But she's much better than expected." Leonie ducked her head.

"I'm sorry. Overload can be very painful, but the results are rarely lasting. I can't imagine how a parent feels when their child is in such jeopardy," Jauffre said.

"Can't you?" Leonie looked up at him. "Walk with me, Jauffre."

"If you'd like." Together they went out through the green doors and across the brightly lit corridor to the glass doors on the other side. The Night Garden was cool and pleasant, smelling of rain and soil, low-light plants growing in fragrant profusion. Their ancestors had used every bit of bio-engineering at their disposal to make Morrigan not only fruitful, but also beautiful.

Leonie led him to a bench beneath an arbor. She sat down, folding her hands in her lap.

"If it is about Elen," Jauffre began, "I am happy to help. I know she said she was a Dreamer, but if she does indeed have electromancer talents, I have trained many young people to use them well. I know Sandrine does not intend to keep the restrictions. I don't think it would be necessary for her to leave Holyrood. We are planning for my apprentices to come here, in fact. But I'm sure this is a shock to you."

Leonie looked up, a rueful expression on her face. "You'd think so, wouldn't you?" She shook her head. "Let me tell you a story about a very ambitious young woman. When I was twenty-six I was certain that I wanted to be Hierophant. I wanted to rise to the highest levels of policy and politics and could see the path before me. This was years before I met my life companion Gilliane. I wanted a child to help me rise. My bloodline isn't prestigious, and I thought that a talented child would improve my reputation. I asked for a match. I was sent a portfolio of twelve possible donors." Leonie picked up a fallen leaf from the bench, turning it over in her hands. Jauffre waited. "Twelve men reduced to numbers and maps of their alleles. And descriptions, of course. I weeded them carefully, removing those who didn't fit my intentions. Tall, because I'm short. Handsome. Intelligent as well as genetically gifted. Well-read, interested in the world, ambitious as I am. And of course extremely talented."

She looked at him, and Jauffre felt his heart speed.

"That the optimal candidate was an electromancer was an acceptable risk. It is easy to make cold choices about a group of cells in a petri dish. It's not a person, after all. And so I chose that donation and had two embryos implanted. One took. That's Elen." She stopped and then went on. "And then she was a person, of course. When people talked about the danger of electromancers, I thought of my beautiful little girl, my Elen with her clever hands and silly jokes, and the idea of anyone taking her from me was intolerable. I prayed to all the gods, I prayed to Blessed Khreesos, that she would be a Dreamer. I prayed she would stay mine."

"Leonie," Jauffre said, and then stopped, uncertain of how to go on.

Leonie looked up, the faint light of the Night Garden illuminating her features. "After the war, Sandrine started pushing Dariah about electromancers, and I joined her. We were the radicals together. *If it were my daughter*....that's a phrase people say, isn't it? But for me it was real. What if Elen manifested? My darling, my spirit, my delight—what if it were her? And so I backed Dariah. I pulled every political string I had. I pushed beside Sandrine. We were a faction, a power. It made Dariah enemies. We know where that led." She glanced at Jauffre.

Jauffre nodded slowly. Seventeen years ago. "Leonie, do you know?"

"Of course I do. I got into the files as soon as I had risen high enough to access them, during the war. I put a name to that number: Jauffre Castal-Edo."

Jauffre tilted his head back, the arbor above obscuring the stars. "I am Elen's progenitor."

"Yes. When Sandrine invited you to court right after the war, I knew. I watched you. I wondered what you were like and I wanted to see. When you demonstrated electromancy for the Archegos, I watched. And I heard Sandrine talk about you. We were close, Sandrine and I. She is one of my dearest friends." Leonie shook her head. "And I could see that she was in love with you. How could I tell her then that I had what she could never have, a child of your body?"

"Elen," he said. Of course. He should have seen it, should have seen it in her face, her quick wits and insouciant smile. He'd thought she was a clever apprentice, mature for her age, but he'd never guessed. And now he knew: her dark hair, her height, the shape of her hands, were all his.

"Elen," Leonie said. "When you were a prisoner here and Sandrine needed to get to the tomb, Elen volunteered to help. How could I refuse her? The man she wanted to save was her own progenitor."

"I wondered that you gave her Windfollower," Jauffre said. He huffed out a deep breath. "Elen opened a door in front of me and I didn't think."

"Elen has always been able to do that. I have pretended, and had her pretend, she did it by ordering the Sema's systems. But we knew she didn't. When we needed to apprehend the Hierarch's accomplices, Elen simply locked them into whatever room they were in by fusing the door mechanisms."

Jauffre smiled. "That's a quick and dirty way, one of the first things electromancers learn. It's easy to teach oneself. I suppose she did."

Leonie nodded. "She taught herself years ago. I knew she could do it. I made her promise me she never would, except when it was vitally necessary. Shorted circuits and fused wires are impossible to hide. Anyone would know it was an electromancer."

"Does Sandrine know?" Jauffre asked.

Leonie shook her head. "Not yet. I haven't told Elen yet either, though it's possible she has guessed. When she was old enough to ask, I told her that her progenitor was an electromancer, a man I had never met who was kind enough to provide the donation because I wanted a baby very much. Nobody knows but me and you. I thought you deserved to hear first. Now that she has done something that cannot be construed as anything but electromancy...."

"By saving thousands of lives in Holyrood," Jauffre pointed out.

"By saving the Sema," Leonie smiled. "My brave girl. Of

course she was willing to die for her family and her friends."

"But she's not dead. And she'll recover from overload. I've done it several times. She'll be fine," Jauffre said.

"She will have to be openly an electromancer, was my point," Leonie said. "Everything I've feared. All the hatred I've tried to keep her from. Being locked away."

"That won't happen," Jauffre said. "She saved the Sema. And the electromancers fought with the Fleet. We'll never go back to the restrictions. And right now Sandrine has the public will behind her. She can make the change. We can thank Calpurnia for that."

Leonie laughed. "I suppose we can. Right now Sandrine could declare night is day and people would cheer."

"If she stands up tomorrow with a beautiful young hero and decorates her for saving thousands of people from being killed by a missile, Elen will never be locked up. And I can send for my apprentices from Sea Easting. And Sai can see his mother."

Leonie bent her head. "Oh."

"He's six and a half. His mother would like to see him too," Jauffre said gently. "And we can make that so."

"We can," Leonie said. She lifted clear, bright eyes. "Will you train Elen? I will need to tell her. And now there is no hiding it. She must be properly trained."

"Of course," Jauffre said. His daughter. And yet one of many. He had raised Boral from infancy, and Verla and Melisande since they were tiny. He'd had Arlaine for six years now. There was room enough for all of them. Love had no upper limit.

Leonie smiled. "I'll tell her today, then."

Jauffre tried to refocus. "Are there other things you need me to do before the investiture tomorrow?"

"Actually get Sandrine there?" Leonie said. "I'm half-afraid she'll bolt. Sandrine isn't very fond of ceremonies. And she certainly can't skip this one or just do an abbreviated form. Also she needs to be decently clothed. I'm not sure she owns anything but uniforms."

"There's nothing wrong with a dress uniform," Jauffre said. "They wanted a martial leader and they got one. I'm sure she has a nice one from being Somatophylax. Simple. Severe."

Leonie smiled. "You do know her, don't you? I am arranging the ceremony. I will trust you to get her there in proper attire."

"You may count on me," Jauffre said.

It had been a very long day. The corridors of the Sema were silent and nearly deserted when Sandrine went to her room, her own room, not the grand suite belonging to the Warlady which had been Dariah's. She supposed she'd have to change rooms after the Investiture, but tonight at least she still had her old room.

Jauffre was waiting for her, propped up in her bed with a screen in his lap, wearing that outrageous scarlet robe. "I hope you don't mind that I let myself in again," Jauffre said. "It's late."

"Stay here with me," she said. How good, how normal, how like old times, to simply come in and find him there. Sandrine changed into her regular night clothes, a black sleeveless shirt and a pair of loose black trousers that were really a bit too long because the hem was torn out. She didn't need to hunt for them. Everything was always exactly where she put it. Nothing was ever out of place in her room. Except Jauffre's things, his clothes strewn on the floor and his boots under the corner of the bed, a used tea bowl on the side table and his bag of personal items on the cabinet. Jauffre no longer lived as though everything had to be stowed for jump. Well, why should he? He'd been on a planet most of the last ten years. And he'd always driven her mad with his sloppiness. Sandrine smiled. It would be good to have that petty irritation back again, her neatness and his untidiness. And he, of course, would ask why her clothes were always falling apart when she could easily replace them. He never had a thread misplaced.

She slid into bed beside him and he put the screen down on the side table. The bed was already warm and it was so good to just put her arms around him. "I've wanted this so many times," she said as he drew her close.

"My heart, my spirit." He held her tight and she laid her cheek against his chest.

"I suppose I'm going to have to move into the Warlady's apartments," she said.

"You sound reluctant."

Sandrine took a deep breath. "They're Dariah's," she said. "Sleeping in her bed, using her things…it will feel so wrong. The reception rooms won't be so bad. It's horribly formal and stiff and there isn't really anything of her in them. And the office is an office—utilitarian."

"Surely her personal things will go to her family," Jauffre said. "I understand she has a son."

"She does. He's a scientist in the west," Sandrine said. "I expect he'll be here tomorrow with his life companion and their daughter." She considered the conversation she'd need to have. It would be painful, but perhaps Leonie could handle Dariah's personal possessions. Leonie was much more comforting than she was. She never knew what to say.

"I'm glad of that," Jauffre said. "But yes, I'm afraid you have to move into the Archegos's official apartments since you're the Archegos."

"Unfortunately, the furniture belongs to the Sema," Sandrine said, thinking of Dariah's rooms, the many times she'd been there.

He craned his neck to look at her. "Surely the Sema has some other furniture."

"Well, yes. Leonie says there are rooms full of things stored in the basement, everything belonging to previous Archegoi that aren't used right now." Sandrine sighed. "I have no time and Leonie will tell you I have no taste."

His hand was warm on her shoulder. "I could look through it and get furniture moved," he said hesitantly.

"Would you?" Sandrine asked. "Jauffre, that would be wonderful."

He looked unexpectedly delighted. "Of course." He ducked his head, kissing her brow. "You like the whole lion's heads and gilt on everything style, yes?"

"Perhaps something more somber," Sandrine said. Jauffre did have a taste for glitter.

"I'll see what I can do," he said. She heard the smile in his voice. "Perhaps the red and black and gold of Argheeros I's era, with lots of canopies and faux animals.... He had a scorpion throne, didn't he? As if he was sitting on the scorpion with its tail rearing up over his head?"

"That is in Abi's play, not in real life," Sandrine said quellingly. "He did not."

"If you say so," Jauffre said.

She shook her head. It would be fine, and if there was more gilt than strictly necessary, it would be historic. "And you," she said. "When you're doing that, I was wondering...." She started over again. "There's a whole suite. I know you need your privacy and it's truly a necessity for you not to feel that you are being watched, but do you think you might want a room and an office in the suite? So that instead of hundreds of kilometers between us, there's only a door?"

"I think that would be ideal," he said, his arms tight around her.

Sandrine closed her eyes. "My love."

"I could take the screens and cameras out," Jauffre said.

"Of course." She understood that. Nothing that was like surveillance.

"And fry the wiring in the walls."

"If you must." The next Archegos would need an electrician.

But that would be their problem, not hers.

"And rooms for my apprentices and a workroom and a classroom…."

She'd seen it coming. "Of course," she said. "There's plenty of space for all your apprentices. Though perhaps not in my suite."

"Maybe not that close," Jauffre said. He waved a hand and the light went off. "I would like a little privacy with you."

"I think we've earned it," Sandrine said. Eleven years, and now at last she could sleep with his arms around her and hide it from no one. "I've dreamed of sleeping beside you for so long."

"And other things," Jauffre said. His finger traced a pattern on her upper arm, just a faint whisper of electricity in it.

Sandrine closed her eyes, biting her lip. "When you do that…."

"Yes?" he said innocently. His finger traced a figure eight.

"You can put more into it than that," she said, feeling the prickle of current more strongly, an insistent purr that went straight to every pleasure center. He drew a pattern across her shoulder, across her collar bones. "More," she said.

"I don't want to leave red marks," Jauffre said. He sounded a little breathless. "There's the ceremony tomorrow."

"The dress uniform has a high collar," Sandrine said.

He laughed. "You always want to dare everything."

"Yes," she said. There was something incredibly arousing about all that power so tightly held. If there was deep hurt as well, no one but her would ever know it. His scars were as dear to her as everything else about him.

His finger traced a pattern of electricity down her breast, her back arching with pleasure. "I will dare anything with you."

"My dear," she said, and gave herself to sensation.

It was quite some time later that they sprawled together, face to face as always, limbs tangled. Since he couldn't bear to be pinned, they shifted so that his head rested on her shoulder. He kissed it. "I'm afraid there are marks."

"Superficial burns," Sandrine said, stroking up his back and tangling her hand in his hair. "Nobody will notice. Completely worth it. The things an electromancer can do…."

"Things I certainly don't teach," Jauffre said.

"That would be indecent." He was loose against her, boneless with release. Sandrine took a deep breath, feeling it all the way to her belly. She was boneless too. "That was what I needed."

"Yes," he said, nuzzling her, sleep in his voice. "Tomorrow is going to be grueling. For you more than me."

Sandrine bent her head, tucking her chin against the top of his head. "I expect so." And yet there was one thing more to arrange. "I don't have a Somatophylax yet. There are a number of strong candidates, but I'm not ready to choose at the moment. I need to talk with each of them about their intentions and their viewpoints."

"That seems like a good idea." Jauffre shifted a little, getting comfortable with her for a pillow. "Is there any reason you have to decide immediately?"

"No, not precipitously," she said. "I will need one in the next weeks, but certainly not tomorrow."

"Then it's better to take your time." He shifted again, managing to steal half the blankets in the process.

Sandrine paused, finding the right words. "Tomorrow, when I am invested as Archegos by the Hierophant, before the College and all the people of Morrigan on the nets, I will not have a Somatophylax to stand at my right hand. Will you stand there?"

She felt his arm tighten around her, and yet his voice was steady. "I'm not sure that's a good idea. An electromancer? That's a lot to ask people to accept."

"I intend to begin as I will go on," Sandrine said. "And it is in part due to the electromancers that Morrigan is still free. I will not hide you. You are not my dirty little secret. You are my companion, as Khreesos's companions were. Stand beside me, Jauffre. Stand beside me for all electromancers."

He pulled her tight against him, holding her to him as though they stood in a howling wind. "Of course I will," he said. "Anything for you, Sandrine."

It was, Jauffre thought, a scene worthy of a play. The Sema glowed with light, fire running down the great troughs in the Antechamber to the Presence, worthies of every type in their best raiment, glowing with jewel colors and gold embroidery. Their chairs formed an aisle from the outer doors to a single ornate chair that stood on the dais before the braziers that guarded the door to the Inner Sanctum.

Someone announced in a loud voice, "See, oh people of Morrigan, your Warlady!"

Sandrine's dark dress uniform was spotless, her hair braided up and her head held high as she walked alone to the dais. When she knelt to receive the Hierophant's blessing, her obeisance was an act of grace and pride. When they laid the Sword of Khreesos in her hands and she kissed the blade, her eyes closed with an expression like ecstasy. Jauffre wondered if she spoke with the Presence, and what he said.

Leonie turned to the assembled room, the cameras catching every angle. "People of Morrigan, the Archegos Sandrine."

Sandrine took two steps and sat gracefully in the black high-backed chair in front of the doors to the Inner Sanctum, one leg forward, the bared sword across her lap. Leonie stood to her left. Sandrine's eyes met his, a smile in them.

Jauffre nodded. A player knows his entrance. He stepped up onto the dais, coming to stand at her right hand, his silver in glimmering contrast to her indigo, and turned to face the people of Morrigan, his head held high. Lightning played in his cupped hands.

Appendix:

Morriganian Fleet Circular

To: Her Graciousness Sandrine Dal-Vesta, Archegos of Morrigan
From: Skir Lin-Hallat, staff assistant to the Warlady
Classification: restricted/draft

Your Graciousness, here is the new draft of Fleet Circular 149 as you requested for your review. — Skir Lin-Hallat

Fleet Circular 149 — Port of Call: Beira on Menaechmi

When visiting a world of such social differences from Morrigan as Menaechmi, it is wise for all Fleet personnel to read and attend to the Circular which explains how not to give offense to the natives of the world we visit. Thus, we begin with the founding of Menaechmi and how it is that their society evolved so differently from ours.

The story begins on the generation ships that brought us to the Nine Worlds. Knowing the limited capacity of the ships and the length of the anticipated voyage, each of the original voyagers from our homeworld consented to reversible sterilization before they embarked. Each ship carried a collection of people from young children to early middle age, and each ship was not filled to capacity. Spaces were left for those of reproductive age to have children, thus eventually creating an optimal distribution of ages throughout the human life cycle. A lottery was inaugurated; each year those who wished to conceive entered the lottery to gain a space. Winners had a year to reverse sterilization and conceive. One might enter the lottery as often as one wished. However, only three completed pregnancies were allowed per individual. Thus, over thirty years, the ships' companies reached capacity and optimal distribution. After that, they operated on "one out, one in"; the number of conceptions in the lottery each year was determined by the number of people who had died, thus maintaining the total population at a viable level.

Rather unreasonably, some voyagers were unhappy with this sensible arrangement, especially in the second and third generation: people who had not themselves consented to the voyage, but whose parents or grandparents had entered into it. They wished to end all breeding restrictions in the name of reproductive freedom, which would obviously have rendered the ecosystems of the ships untenable. Thus, when the voyagers reached the world of Menaechmi, many were eager to stay.

With broad oceans and twin suns, Menaechmi is hot and its diurnal cycle is challenging. Yet no fewer than twenty percent of the voyagers elected to end their travels. They immediately threw out all the restrictions. To this day, all but a small minority population in the interior of Menaechmi's single large continent practice free breeding. Anyone can reproduce with anyone else, either through spontaneous copulation or through assisted means which are only scantily regulated. There are no mandatory genetic screenings. On Morrigan no defective embryos are ever implanted, and over the centuries most congenital illnesses have been removed from the gene pool. No one is born with a disability. In stark contrast, Menaechmi allows, either through inattention or the misplaced idea that genetic defects are somehow inevitable, any conception that the individual conceiving does not actively prevent. The only taboo seems to be incest, which Menaechmans carry to extremes: liaisons with second cousins, step-siblings with no blood relationship, and even members of the same House are looked on askance even if the relationship is distant or non-genetic.

You are missing the point of a Fleet Circular. This is being read by a twenty-year-old on their way to a bar. No need to go back to the Voyagers. Also they are not conceiving with relatives on Menaechmi. Cut to what they need to know. Pick up here. —Sandrine Dal-Vesta

While assignations are common among adults on Morrigan, either at one's home or at Red Houses where a casual or more serious meeting can occur, this is not true of Menaechmi. There is no equivalent of the Red House, that comfortable and private setting where those in communal housing or who live with family members can enjoy an hour or an evening with someone. To begin with, prostitution is legal on Menaechmi, and the inviting people who are eager to make acquaintance are not friendly locals, but plying this trade. At some point in the negotiations, they will whip out a hand-held and expect you to tick the boxes of their contract, detailing what services will be provided, for how long, and for what amount of currency. Visitors must read the contract carefully. There may be unique stipulations that are not agreeable, or it may simply involve more currency than expected! While it is certainly not against Fleet regulations to enter into a short contract while on Menaechmi, all of our Fleet personnel being adults of responsible age whose sexual expression is their own business, buyer beware! Your captain will not appreciate an appearance before a magisterial court.

Your captain certainly will not. —SDV

Even though there is little chance of a conception if you have proper implants to prevent production of genetically viable material, it is true that nothing is foolproof. It's important to understand that any child who is the product of free breeding will not be recognized on Morrigan, will have no place in the blood hierarchy, and will not be a citizen. They will be Menaechman legally and culturally. Unlike our more casual companionship, which does not necessarily have any legal force unless the parties to it so decide, it is possible to enter into a long-term contract that is legally binding and provides the other party with kinship rights. Therefore, if you should desire to enter into a matrimonial contract or one intended to produce progeny….

They are on Menaechmi for a port call! They are not entering into a matrimonial contract! Cut to the part that applies to a port call. —SDV

Generally speaking, and odder to our eyes, most of these liaisons are expected to occur in what we would consider public spaces: a curtained alcove off a club area, a balcony above a casino room, or a tent on the beach. Morriganians may find this disconcerting. Menaechmans do not have sex in sleeping areas. If you rent a hotel room, it will be a small space meant for sleeping and escorts will not accompany you there. Nor should you accompany an escort far from most public areas, as it is not unheard of for escorts to lead marks to where they can be robbed. It's best to confine oneself to licensed professionals in resort areas.

Are we really telling them how to hire prostitutes? Too much detail. —SDV

In terms of other entertainment…

Yes, please. The Fleet does do something besides have sex. —SDV

…Menaechmi and the port of Beira provide many opportunities for cultural exchange. Performing arts are greatly prized, just as they are on Morrigan. Live music, dance and theater are common, and there are many inexpensive venues near the starport which offer hours of entertainment for a small cover charge and the price of drinks. Intoxicants are common and unregulated. While we have strict standards about what percentage of alcohol or other intoxicants must be identified, on Menaechmi many drinks or foodstuffs may not identify ingredients. If in doubt, it is best to ask and to buy drinks or foodstuffs only from respectable establishments. There is a Guild system that regulates the use of certain terms, but its intricacies are opaque to an outsider without a thorough explanation of viticulture and agavefabricia.

Now we are telling them how to buy wine? Cut the next part. They do not need to know how to judge varieties of spirits. —SDV

Beira is known for its beautiful beaches as well as its nightlife. It is tempting to enjoy white sand, warm water, and abundant sunshine, but remember the sun is not our friend! It's possible to get a serious sunburn in less than half an hour, or to get sun poisoning or severe burns in an hour. Always wear appropriate prophylactics and sun-block clothing. While you may see locals swimming nude, even children and elders, do not attempt this unless it is for a very brief period or under a sun-block awning. (There are some beach clubs that provide shades that extend into shallow water.) Because all human habitation on Morrigan is on the night side, you are not used to it, have not had various skin treatments, and do not have the products that locals use lavishly to prevent burns. While some topical solutions are available at beach stands, use with caution. You do not know how you will react to them. It is best to wear clothing that covers the entire body and to wear full-spectrum light-blocking glasses.

You will look like a freak on the beach, but that is a hazard. Yes, they swim nude, and "clothing" on the beach does not cover much. Your captain will also not appreciate having to retrieve you from a clinic where you have been taken with sun poisoning. —SDV

In terms of entertainment venues, there are many that provide games of chance. However, be aware that these games are weighted in favor of the house, and that virgin players are more likely to lose money than win it.

Really? As though there is no gambling in the Fleet? —SDV

In short, while a port call at Beira on Menaechmi may offer opportunities for personal enrichment, it may also offer many hazards.

As does life. —SDV

Acknowledgments

The author would like to extend her thanks to those who kindly read and commented on *Warlady* before its publication: Victoria Francis, Melissa Scott, Lena Strid and my wonderful partner, Amy Griswold. I would also like to thank my editor, Athena Andreadis, who has improved *Warlady* immeasurably with her editorial suggestions.

ABOUT THE AUTHOR

Jo Graham is the author of twenty-five books and three online games. Best known for her historical fantasy novels *Black Ships* and *Stealing Fire*, and her tie-in novels for MGM's popular *Stargate: Atlantis* and *Stargate: SG1* series, she has been a Locus Award finalist, an Amazon Top Choice, a Spectrum Award finalist, a Romantic Times Top Pick in historical fiction and a Lambda Literary Award and Rainbow Award nominee for bisexual fiction. With Melissa Scott, she is the author of five books in the *Order of the Air* series, a historical fantasy series set in the 1920s and 30s. She is also the author of two pagan spirituality books. She lives in North Carolina with her partner and is the mother of two daughters.